TIGER BOY

TIGER BOY

MITALI PERKINS

Charlesbridge

First paperback edition 2017
Text copyright © 2015 by Mitali Perkins
Illustrations copyright © 2017 by Tanvi Bhat
All rights reserved, including the right of reproduction in whole or in part in any form.
Charlesbridge and colophon are registered trademarks of Charlesbridge Publishing, Inc.

Published by Charlesbridge
85 Main Street
Watertown, MA 02472
(617) 926-0329
www.charlesbridge.com

Library of Congress Cataloging-in-Publication Data available upon request.
 ISBN 978-1-58089-660-3 (reinforced for library use)
 ISBN 978-1-58089-661-0 (softcover)
 ISBN 978-1-60734-543-5 (ebook)
 ISBN 978-1-60734-664-7 (ebook pdf)

Printed in the United States of America
(hc) 10 9 8 7 6 5 4 3 2 1
(sc) 10 9 8 7 6 5 4 3 2 1

Digital illustrations inspired by patachitra, a type of Bengali folk art
Display type set in Carrotflower by Tart Workshop
Text type set in Adobe Caslon by Adobe Systems Incorporated
Printed by Berryville Graphics in Berryville, Virginia, USA
Production supervision by Brian G. Walker
Designed by Diane M. Earley
Paperback designed by Sarah Richards Taylor

For Nikhil and Ranju

—M. P.

TIGER BOY

one

SPLASH! SPLASH! The two boys stripped off their school uniforms and jumped into the pond. Their heads bobbed as they wrestled and dunked each other.

"Race you!" called Ajay.

Neel swam behind his lanky friend, feeling as sleek and fast as a river dolphin, even though he was sure to lose. It had been much warmer than usual for January, and it was three o'clock, the hottest part of the day. *I should be home studying*, he thought. Teacher was concerned about how behind Neel was in his preparation. The big exam was in April, and Neel's math skills weren't getting better.

The pond was a short detour from the path around

the island, about halfway between school and home. How good it felt to drop his heavy satchel, unbutton the starched white shirt, tear off those stiff school shorts, and jump into the refreshing water!

This pond was freshwater, but most of the creeks and rivers in the Sunderbans were salty and muddy. Neel didn't mind—he loved the tang of salt on his tongue and the squish of mud between his toes. Home for him was the hiss of his father's boat as it slipped through the deltas, *golpata* branches swaying in the monsoon rains, and the evening smell of jasmine flowers near his house mingling with green chilies and fresh *ilish* fish simmering in mustard-seed oil. Neel had climbed all the tall palm trees, waded in the creeks, and foraged for wild guavas in every corner of the mangrove forest.

Ajay was already stretched out on the muddy bank at the far side of the pond, pretending to be asleep. He lifted his head and smirked at Neel.

Neel's feet touched bottom again and he waded to the bank. He didn't really mind losing to his friend. Ajay had always been fast and agile in ponds and on the cricket field, but that didn't seem to matter much in their village. Boys were supposed to do well in school, not on the sports field. Ajay's father taught Class Two, despairing that his own son was one of the slowest to learn inside a classroom.

"I miss Viju," Neel said, plopping down beside Ajay. "I beat him once, remember?"

"When we were four years old," said Ajay. He dodged to avoid the scoop of mud Neel flipped his way.

"I thought he might start going to school again now that his father's back from Chennai."

"Me, too. Maybe they're fishing together."

Neel sighed—fishing all day sounded like bliss compared to wearing a hot, scratchy uniform and struggling with math problems. "I'm sure he's getting good at it. Do you think he's inside the reserve?"

"No chance. It's too dangerous for someone our age to go behind the fence."

"I think he is," Neel said. "There's not enough fish left anywhere else, that's for sure. Not since the cyclone hit. When Baba takes his boat into the reserve, he comes back with plenty. And honey, too."

"But the tigers are hungrier now," said Ajay. He was right. Villagers like Baba ventured behind the nylon-mesh fence into the reserve at their own risk. If a man—or boy—was seized by a tiger, he would be dragged off into the forest and eaten. Tigers had already claimed five victims from their island this year.

"I don't see why Viju's father needs to fish anyway," Neel said. "He's making all that money working for greedy Gupta."

Gupta was a newcomer to the Sunderbans, but he acted like he owned the entire island. The bad news was that these days, he almost did. After the cyclone hit, many of the men and older boys, and even some of the girls, had left to find work in faraway cities. Viju's father had come back, but others had never returned. Sometimes their families didn't hear from them again and were forced to sell parcels of land to Gupta.

Ajay stood up. "One more race? I like beating the smartest kid in school at something."

"Pretend a crocodile's chasing you," Neel said. "I'm in no rush."

He pushed away the thought of the math assignments in his satchel, floated on his back, and watched wispy white clouds chase each other across the wide blue sky. "We named you after my favorite color, Neel," Ma often said, pointing at the horizon where the blue of the sky met the blue of the water. Humming one of his mother's favorite songs, Neel imagined what it would be like to venture deep into the reserve to hunt for honey, or to pole a boat into an inlet where tiger tracks lined the muddy banks. Baba had never taken Neel to the reserve. "Too dangerous, Son," he answered whenever Neel asked. "We have to protect that smart brain of yours from claws and teeth."

"Well, what about your brain, Baba?" Neel always responded.

"Mine isn't as good as the one in here," Baba would say, gently rapping Neel's skull with his knuckles.

Suddenly a familiar shout came from the *golpata* trees. Lickety-split, a boy hurtled to the pond, stripped to his underwear, and leaped into the water. It was Viju! Immediately Neel and Ajay pounced and pushed him under.

After a minute or two, Viju pulled away from the scuffle. "Let's dry off. I've got some big news."

"Huge catch of fish, maybe?" Ajay asked.

Neel felt a twinge of jealousy. "I bet you saw a tiger!"

"I'll tell you everything—don't worry. I need your help, in fact."

The boys swam to the stone ledge where they'd left their clothes, climbed out of the water, and squatted in the sunshine.

"Well?" asked Neel.

"Actually I did see a tiger, but that's not my news," Viju said.

"You *did*?"

"Where? When?"

"In the reserve. It was just a flash of orange and black through the trees. I was alone; my *baba* hadn't come back yet."

"Behind the fence? Weren't you scared?" Ajay shook his head so that drops of water flew everywhere. "I'd have fainted dead of fright, right then and there. One quick tiger snack—that's me."

"What did you do?" Neel asked, trying to imagine himself in Viju's place.

"Dropped my net, jumped into the boat, and rowed out as fast as I could. I'm glad I don't have to try that again now that my *baba's* back. I'm helping him these days—he's making real money."

Dirty money, you mean, thought Neel, but he didn't say it aloud. Gupta paid his workers stacks of rupees to threaten tenants who fell behind on their rent. He hired others to cut down rare *sundari* trees that grew on the uninhabited islands of the reserve. Sadly, these days even Neel's father needed the extra income. After fishing and foraging in the mornings for the family, Baba was doing carpentry for Gupta in the afternoons. Neel was sure, though, that his father would never do anything like demand money from widows who used to own their land.

"Want to hear my *big* news?" Viju asked, lowering his voice and glancing around as if he were afraid someone might be listening.

"Well, what is it?" Ajay asked.

Viju hesitated. "You have to keep it a secret. Do you promise, Ajay?"

"Fine."

"Neel?" Viju asked.

"Yes, yes. Hurry up and tell us."

"One of the new tiger cubs has escaped!"

two

BOTH AJAY AND NEEL GASPED. This *was* big news. The reserve's hungry, thin female tigers gave birth so rarely nowadays. When three cubs were born ten weeks ago, rangers visited all fifty or so of the inhabited islands to share the good news. Grateful villagers offered extra sweets and flowers to their statues of Bon Bibi, protector of the Sunderbans. When word came that one of the babies had died, the whole island mourned. Now only two were left.

Neel leaned forward in excitement. "How did it get out? Was it the boy or girl cub? Where do they think it is now?" Imagine seeing a tiger cub with his own eyes!

"One question at a time!" Viju said. "It clawed a small hole in the fence. Don't worry—they fixed it. And I have no idea if it's the girl or boy. And as for where it is? Get this—they say it's *on our island.* They don't know exactly where."

"*Here?*" Ajay jumped to his feet as if an enormous man-eater were about to pounce.

"Relax," Viju said. "It's still tiny. Ten weeks old. Not much bigger than a small cat."

"But how do they know it's here?" Neel asked. He could hardly believe it. A tiger cub, on their island!

"Fishermen spotted small pugmarks on the shore, leading across the path into the mangrove forest."

Ajay grabbed his clothes. "Pugmarks? You know what they say—big paw prints follow small ones. That mother tiger's going to escape, and then she'll swim right over here to find her cub."

"That's why *we* have to find it first," said Viju, ignoring Ajay and edging a little closer to Neel. "And anyway, here's the secret part. My father and I need your help, Neel. Nobody knows the hiding places on this island better than you. Gupta's offered a big reward to anyone who finds the cub. No questions asked, no tales told."

"Not a chance!" cried Neel. "I'm not hunting a tiger cub for Gupta."

Viju put a hand on his arm. "Shhh, Neel! Keep your voice down!"

Neel yanked his arm away and stood up. "I don't care who hears me. That man will make a fortune selling that poor cub's skin on the black market. And its body parts for medicine. Who wants to fill a greedy man's pockets with more cash?"

"Not me," said Ajay. "That Gupta's more dangerous than a tiger."

"I'm going right now to tell the rangers," Neel said, pulling on his shorts.

"You can't!" Viju leaped to his feet, eyes widening in alarm. "Gupta's men will beat me up. And you, too, probably. Besides, my father will lose his job—he's getting paid to search for the cub. You can't say anything! Promise me you won't. Not even to your families."

Neel caught Ajay's eye, and Ajay shrugged. The three of them had been friends since they were small. When Viju's father was in Chennai, Neel could remember watching their friend's hair become straw-colored from hunger. Both he and Ajay had shared food with Viju during that time. "OK," Neel said reluctantly. "But if I find the cub first, I'm taking it straight to the rangers."

"Me, too," said Ajay.

The boys were silent as they finished getting dressed. Neel's stomach was churning. *Gupta's taken over our island, and now he wants our tigers, too? Someone has to stop him!* If only Neel could tell Baba about this . . . but Viju seemed so desperate.

Just as Neel was buttoning the last button on his shirt, the *golpata* trees rustled behind them.

"What?! Can I believe my eyes?"

Neel jumped. Turning, he saw the worst possible person to catch him swimming after school: Headmaster, shaking a fist in their direction. Why was *he* taking a detour on this edge of the island, so far from school?

Headmaster stalked over and grabbed Neel's shoulder with an iron grip, ignoring the two other boys. Viju and Ajay seized the chance and bolted, and Neel couldn't blame them. Viju was already in trouble for dropping out of school. And Headmaster would probably heap the blame for any of Ajay's misdeeds on Ajay's father's head.

Headmaster gave Neel a shake. "Playing? Wait until your father hears about this. I was on my way to tell him about your disgusting lack of effort, and this escapade of yours will prove my case. I assume he's at home?"

"N—no, sir," stammered Neel.

"Well, where is he, then?" Headmaster asked. The metal fingers didn't budge.

"He's working on a new building, sir."

Headmaster raised his eyebrows. "A new building? On this side of the island? Who's the owner?"

"Mr. Gupta, sir."

"Rich man? New around here?"

"That—that's him, sir."

"Another person I want to see. Will he be at the building site?"

"I think so—I mean I think so, *sir*."

"Let's go, then. Take me there. How do you say it in English? I'll . . . er . . . 'murder two birds with the same rock.'" Thanks to his studies in London, Headmaster often shifted back and forth between Bangla and English, but he always seemed to mangle English proverbs and expressions.

Neel's heart was still hammering from the shock of Headmaster's appearance, but he corrected the mistake in his head: *Kill two birds with one stone.* New words and phrases in any language sank deeply into Neel's mind and stayed there. Often, during recess, while the other boys played outside, Neel devoured Bangla poetry and English novels that he found in the school's small library. He had started reading almost as soon as he entered school, struggling at first through the English books by looking up words and phrases in the big dictionary. Now that he was in Class Five, English came to him almost as readily as Bangla. He'd read all the books at the school, but every week a new stack of unread magazines, books, and newspapers appeared in the library as though they were waiting for him. It was like magic. He didn't know where they came from, but he read them from cover to cover and eagerly waited for the next batch.

Headmaster pushed Neel back through the low-hanging branches that bordered the narrow path to the pond. They crossed a small bamboo bridge spanning one of the many creeks that curved in through the muddy banks of the island. When they reached the wide, raised path that circled the whole outer rim of the island, Headmaster stopped to catch his breath.

Neel strained to hear the sound of a soft mew of a cub, but the chatter of the rhesus monkeys and Headmaster's loud panting made it impossible to hear anything else. Where could the cub be? Maybe Gupta's men had already captured it, or it had been discovered by a crocodile. Anything could happen to a young creature far from home.

three

COMING AROUND A BEND, they heard voices approaching on the path, and three rangers carrying rifles came into sight. Dressed in forest green, they were wearing helmets designed to fend off tiger attacks—metal shields covered the backs of their necks. Neel studied them closely; it wasn't often that rangers came to their island. The last time had been to make the announcement about the cubs' birth ten weeks ago.

"Good afternoon, sir," said the man in front. He elbowed the two men on either side of him, and they, too, saluted Headmaster.

Headmaster nodded. "Why are you out and about on our island, Kushal?"

"A tiger cub escaped, sir. We think she may be hiding here, and we're asking the islanders to help us find her."

So it's the girl, Neel thought.

"And how did you let that happen?"

"Er ... er ... it was a poor mending job on the fence, sir. Don't worry—I've sacked that worker already."

Headmaster scowled. "I hope you, as the leader, took full responsibility for the mistake. Isn't that what we tried to teach you in school?"

"Yes, sir. I did—I will."

Neel felt a bit better about his own difficulties with Headmaster. This grown man, carrying a rifle and obviously in charge of the others, was squirming like a Class Two student.

"You used to be somewhat intelligent, Kushal." Headmaster pulled Neel forward. "Not quite as bright as this one here, and not half as good at learning English, but a much harder worker. I hear we have only two hundred or so tigers left in the reserve. And now you've lost a cub? Who is guarding the others?"

"We have one man on base, sir." The head ranger turned to Neel. "If a full-grown tiger came to your island, we'd have to hunt her down and tranquilize her. But this is a baby, so we're counting on you islanders to find her. She's not dangerous. She'll come to you after a while if you offer her some food, and once she does, she's easy to carry. Still has her baby teeth, and her claws won't hurt you. Bring her straight to our headquarters. Spread the word, will you?"

Bring all your men! You have to find her now! Gupta's going to sell her on the black market! But he had promised Viju. Neel clamped his lips shut and nodded. Somehow he'd have to find that cub on his own.

"Keep a sharp eye out for pugmarks, small and big," another ranger added. "In the meantime we'll do our best to keep the mother inside the reserve, but she's frantic to find her missing baby."

"I'm sure you have learned from your error," said Headmaster. He turned to Kushal. "You won't let another tiger escape, will you, Son?"

The head ranger shook his head vehemently. "It will never happen again, sir. But we have to get back and make sure there aren't more tears in the fence. It's been a pleasure to see you. I'll never forget all you did—"

Headmaster held up his hand, palm out. "That's enough, Kushal. There's a missing cub out there. Go and spread the news about how to find her. And keep the other tigers safe, will you? We need even more tigers to lure tourists—*and* their rupees—to the Sunderbans."

"Yes, sir!" With one last salute to Headmaster, the rangers hurried down the path.

"Let's go, boy. As they say in England, 'A moving pebble doesn't get covered with dirt.'"

A rolling stone gathers no moss. Neel never said the corrections out loud. Correcting him was unthinkable.

What was Headmaster planning to say to Baba? Neel had seen the delight and pride on his parents' faces when he'd read them the letter:

> *I have selected your son to compete against students from all the other schools in the region for the prestigious Sunderbans Scholarship. The scholarship pays for the top-scoring student in the region to study at a private boarding school in Kolkata. Our school has not had a winner of this competition in recent years, but your son, Neel, is the brightest student I have seen in my tenure here. His grasp of English and Bangla is superior. We will work with him in mathematics to increase his understanding of that subject. It is our earnest expectation that you will do all you can to help your son seize this opportunity.*
> *Yours truly,*
> *Headmaster Arjun Sen*

Neel's voice had dwindled almost to a mumble as he'd read the letter aloud. He had no desire to study in the big city of Kolkata. Why would he want to live anywhere but the island? He could never leave Ma and her delicious cooking; his sister, Rupa, who coddled and teased him; and Baba, who protected and provided for all of them. The sights, sounds, and smells of the Sunderbans were as much a part of him as his dark skin and curly black hair.

But Headmaster ruled the school like the prime minister ruled India—nobody said no to his decisions. The exam was in twelve weeks, and Neel lugged home piles of extra geometry problems that made his tired brain feel as thick and sticky as mud. Not that he worked too hard. He went through the motions, but he certainly didn't intend to win that scholarship. He'd have to take the exam, of course, but then he planned to start secondary school right here in the Sunderbans, on a neighboring island that was just a quick ferry ride away.

He did feel a twinge of guilt when he pictured his parents' disappointment. Would Baba be angry when Headmaster told him how little Neel had been trying? Baba had never lost his temper with Neel or his sister, but there was a first for everything. Today, when Baba heard about Neel swimming with his friends instead of studying, would he give his son the kind of punishment Viju and Ajay often endured—no dinner, a slap or two, even a beating with a stick?

The raised dirt path that wound around the island was bolstered by bags of sand to prevent any more of the shore from disappearing into the water. Villagers had planted new mangrove plants to replace the bushes and trees torn away by the cyclone, and new roots were beginning to push through the salty soil. Dinghies, fishing boats, and other *nauka* passed in the water, and shrimp fishermen trawled blue nets along the shore. Boatmen and passengers alike called loud greetings to Headmaster, who lifted a hand in answer. On the far side of the waterway, the bright orange mesh fence barricaded the islands of the reserve. *I wonder where the cub broke through*, Neel thought. *It's a long swim for a baby, but she made it and landed on a bank somewhere along here.*

To the right they passed patches of mangrove forest and small parcels of land, rice paddies, and chili pepper fields. Neel kept his eyes open for any small pugmarks leading off the path, but Headmaster was hurrying him along. Soon they were in view of Neel's house, where his mother and Rupa were outside in a sunny corner, hanging clothes on the line. Theirs was the only property for kilometers where a grove of tall *sundari* trees provided shade for the house and most of the yard. The trees were aptly named after beauty—their wood wasn't just supple and strong, it was a lovely, glowing red. Baba had planted the grove when Neel was a baby, and he guarded the family trees fiercely from woodcutters. As if in thanks, the sturdy trees had protected their house and fields from the brunt of the cyclone. Because the trees' strong roots had kept the soil in place, the paddies would produce rice this coming harvest. Most of the other farmers would have to wait for another planting cycle.

Neel could see Ma sweeping the area around the outdoor stove where she and Rupa cooked, near where the family gathered to eat. She was moving slowly; it had only been a few days since she'd been able to get up after being sick with dysentery. She didn't catch sight of Headmaster hurrying Neel along the path, but Rupa's head swiveled, her mouth fell open, and she dropped the towel she was wringing. Two black baby goats bleated at Neel from the pen attached to the family's thatch-roofed clay hut, a rooster joined in with a loud crow, and the huddle of hens clucked their worry from the shade of the grove of *sundari* trees.

Headmaster stopped at a small shack that sold homemade goodies, this time to guzzle the juice of a coconut. "It's so blazing hot for January. I'll sweat to death, I'm sure. Our climate is changing due to the rest of the world, and we're the ones who suffer. How much farther?"

"We're close, sir. Just near that tall tree."

four

THE DOCK WAS SURROUNDED by anchored *nauka* bobbing in the current. Boatmen unloaded baskets of wares for customers who would come later in the evening to haggle over prices in the nearby market. Safely away from the bustle of the dock, in the shade of a large tamarind tree, a clearing marked the site for Gupta's new house. The building was to be one of the biggest on the island, made with bricks and wood instead of clay and thatch.

Several men were scattered across the building site. Neel glanced around and spotted his father. Baba was bending over a large pile of wood, which he seemed to be carving as part of a wide veranda on the new building. Was that *sundari* wood? It was. Neel couldn't believe it—usually Baba's was one of the loudest voices on the island protesting the cutting of *sundari* trees. Some of Gupta's men must have risked their lives deep in the reserve to gather such a big amount of the red, sturdy branches. Surely Baba hadn't joined them. *The cost of Ma's medicine and doctor visit must be really high*, Neel thought. He had known that money was short, but he hadn't realized Baba was in such a tight situation.

Gupta, a balding, plump man smoking a fat cigar, was shouting at a foreman. A servant held an umbrella aloft to keep Gupta in the shade, but the burly foreman was sweating in the sunshine. Neel's stomach coiled like a cobra—how could a big, powerful man like Gupta hunt down a defenseless tiger cub?

Gupta caught sight of Headmaster and stopped his tirade. He whispered to his servant, cocked his head to listen, and then lifted a hand to wave. "Delighted to see you, Headmaster!" he called. "I'll be with you shortly."

Headmaster cupped his hands around his mouth. "Jai, come here!" he barked, and Neel remembered that Headmaster had taught the little-boy version of Baba years ago.

Baba turned to see who was calling. Immediately he rose and walked over, wiping his hands on his shirt. A trio of curious bricklayers followed. Baba raised his eyebrows when he caught sight of Neel.

"Good to see you, Headmaster, sir," said Baba. "How might I help you?"

"I sent a letter a few months back about your son competing for the scholarship in Kolkata," Headmaster said. "Did you read it?"

"Yes, sir."

Headmaster's eyes raked Baba's muddy sandals and torn shirt. "*Could* you read it?"

Baba hesitated for a second. "Neel read it to me, sir."

"This is exactly why I scolded *your* father for pulling you out of school before you learned to read. Didn't the contents of my letter explain the extent of study your son must undertake to win this prestigious scholarship?"

"Yes, sir. We're grateful to you for selecting him."

"Do you understand, Jai, that graduates of the school in Kolkata where your son would study have taken top positions everywhere in the world? San Francisco, Mumbai, New York, London, Dubai— these people are changing the world!"

The world maybe, but not my island, thought Neel.

"I understand, sir," said Baba. "I am sure he can win this scholarship."

"Not if he doesn't try. He is making absolutely no progress in math. And today I caught him swimming in the pond after school—as if he doesn't have a care in the world! It's virtually impossible to teach a boy who doesn't want to learn. The only solution for your family at this late date is to hire a top tutor—a miracle worker, in fact. I know of one such man in Kolkata, but it would be expensive to bring him here. Do you have the money?"

Neel could see the other men smirking. They were jealous of Baba's carpentry skills, which earned a higher pay than their work of laying bricks, and of how quickly his rice harvest had recovered. They were enjoying this spectacle.

Baba threw a quick glance at Neel and took a deep breath, as if the next words were hard to utter. "I'm afraid we don't, sir."

"Well, you have this job, don't you?"

Baba's jaw was set, and a muscle in his cheek was twitching. "I'm paying back a bit of debt. My wife fell sick, and we had to pay the doctor and buy medicine."

"Oh! So you're borrowing money. Another poor practice to teach your son."

Baba was silent. Neel wished his father would shout at Headmaster, but Baba never lost his temper. "Angry answers hinder God's purposes," he often said.

Neel yelled at Headmaster in his head: *If Baba spoke English, he'd never make such stupid mistakes!* There were so many things a boy could think but never say to his elders.

Headmaster groaned. "It's too late now to submit another name for the competition." He turned to Neel. "You *must* start trying, boy. You're going to bring shame to our whole village."

"I'm sure he will put his mind to the task of studying hard now, sir," Baba said.

Gupta was walking over, still shadowed by his umbrella-bearing servant. Yanking the cigar stub out of his mouth, he handed it to the servant, who crushed it under his sandaled foot. "Headmaster! What an honor to receive you on this side of our island. I've been wanting to meet you. I am Mr. Gupta. What might I do for you, sir?"

"Ah, these boys will be the death of me. But they are the future of the Sunderbans, you know, and we must invest in their education. We have big plans for our school, so I'm glad a visionary man like you has come to invest in our island. As the English like to say, 'Two brains are two times as strong as one brain.'"

Two heads are better than one, Neel thought, gritting his teeth. The botched proverb grated on his already raw nerves.

Gupta smiled, flashing yellow teeth that reminded Neel of a crocodile. "Come, join me for tea, Headmaster. I'll arrange for a rickshaw to take you back. My, what a dedicated fellow you are!"

The servant hoisted the umbrella higher so that Headmaster could join Gupta under the portable shade. The two men walked toward the tamarind tree, chatting and laughing like old friends.

Baba drew Neel closer, turning his back to the bricklayers. "Son, *have* you been studying wholeheartedly? This scholarship is a chance to have a different kind of future. A life of hard labor—is that what you want? For your hands to look like this?" He held his hands in front of Neel's face.

Neel flinched. "Yes, Baba—" he started.

"You! Enough jabbering." It was the foreman. "Gupta isn't paying you to chat with your lazy son."

Neel saw Baba's fists clench and unclench. Though scarred and cracked, they were sculpted from years of hammering, chiseling, and fishing, and were twice the size of the foreman's. One swing could flatten any man on the island. But Baba didn't speak as he strode back to his work. And he didn't look Neel's way again.

five

NEEL THREW ONE LAST SCOWL at Headmaster and Gupta, who were sipping tea in the shade of the tamarind tree. At first he walked fast to vent his fury, but soon he slowed and began to push aside bushes and leaves. The thought of the small cub far from home and hungry, at the mercy of Gupta's men, was unbearable. She had to get back to the reserve before she was killed and skinned, with each of her body parts sold on the black market to line that rich man's pockets with even more rupees. Maybe someone who didn't know about the reward would find her first, but Neel knew how fast gossip spread on the island. How many people were desperate enough to be tempted by the money?

He didn't expect to see small pugmarks along the banks of the rivulets and creeks, because two high tides and two low tides swept in and out every day. It was low tide now, so he was able to take short detours into the dense patches of mangrove plants that lined the small creeks and inlets, but there was still no sign of the cub. And now Neel was almost home, where he'd have to face his mother and sister and tell them what had happened. He dawdled at the outhouse and took a long time to wash his face, hands, and feet at the pump.

"What did Headmaster want with you?" Rupa demanded as soon as he walked in the doorway.

Neel kept his eyes on his sandals as he left them on the flat stone threshold. Ma was standing next to his sister, waiting for his answer. *Might as well tell them now*, he thought, *before Baba gets home and things get even worse.* "He thinks I'm not learning enough math—that I won't do well on the exam."

"Ay-yo!" Ma wailed. "You have to win that scholarship, Neel! A good education in Kolkata will save our family! Do you see how hard your father works to put rice on our plates? You could get a good job, take care of all of us!" She hurried to the small shrine in the back of the hut, lit an incense stick, and began chanting prayers to the statue of Bon Bibi that always stood there.

"Get out of that dirty uniform," Rupa said, "and then we need to talk."

Neel slipped behind the long sari that divided the room diagonally. Another shorter sari cut the back half in two. Ma and Baba slept on mats in the quarter of the hut that also sheltered the family shrine, and Rupa slept on a mat in the other quarter, along with three boxes full of extra pots and pans, flashlights, soap, toothpaste, cooking oil, spices, and other supplies. Neel had been given the entire front half of the hut for sleeping and studying late into the night. The clean, sleeveless white undershirt and cotton pants his sister left for him after school were folded on her mat. He changed quickly and came back out.

Rupa tossed the dirty uniform onto the threshold, looking ready to launch into one of her sisterly lectures. Neel tried to forestall it by blurting out the news about the cub. But not all of it, even though he usually told his sister everything. He could barely restrain himself from sharing the secret of Gupta's hunt. By picturing the fear in Viju's eyes, though, he managed it. "And there are crocodiles out there!" he ended.

"Poor baby," Rupa said. "Far from home. She must be so scared."

"The rangers said she would be easy to carry," Neel said. "You and I should look, too. The two of us can find her, Didi." His first word years ago had been *didi*, or "older sister."

"We might, but you can't waste any more time doing anything but studying. I'll keep my eyes open— I promise." She sighed and picked up the broom that stood in the corner near Baba's pile of *sundari* wood. The broom was short, made of thin sticks that were tied together. "Did Headmaster take you to Baba and scold you in front of everybody?"

"He didn't say much to me," Neel answered, swallowing. "He . . . he blamed Baba, Didi. It was so awful."

"It must have been! And it's not even his fault! I know you don't study, Neel. You sit here daydreaming every afternoon. I'd give my whole dowry to go to that school in Kolkata—every single bangle, sari, and necklace. And you don't want to even try?"

Neel didn't answer. His sister had stopped going to school after Class Four—Ma had been sick then, too, and had needed her help. Rupa bent to sweep the floor in tidy arcs, lifting the longer sari draped across the room and ducking under it to reach the far corners of the one-room hut.

Neel slumped on the small chair that Baba had built with wood from their trees. The chair was sturdy, solid, and just his size. The matching desk was built carefully at the right height and slant. At school his back ached from sitting in a stiff chair, and the desks were so rickety it was a challenge to write neatly. But at home he could sit in comfort. Baba had even carved flowers and leaves into the wood. These two pieces were the only wooden furniture in the hut—the supply boxes in Rupa's quarter were made of cardboard. Even the gold and jewelry Ma and Baba had saved over the years to give to Rupa's future in-laws as a dowry present were in a cardboard box, although that one was tied securely with thick rope.

Rupa's sweeping had reached Neel's feet, and he lifted them so she could continue. Instead she stopped, straightened, and pointed to his books with her broom. "You spend so many hours sitting there every day, Neel. You must be learning something!"

"Not math. I hate math so much. My brain has a big math block."

"More like a 'leaving home' block, I think."

"I don't want to leave home, Didi. Would you?"

"Of course I would! You could come back, you know." She swept the pile under his feet and guided the dust toward the open door.

"Why would I leave when you're such a good cook?" he asked, smiling. "Dinner's a long time away, and I'm hungry, Didi."

She smiled. "You don't need compliments to get leftovers. You know I always keep some for you."

She swept the dust outside and returned with a small pot of rice and lentils, still warm from the midday meal. Neel ate the small helping in three gulps, and Rupa handed him a wet cloth to wipe his fingers. "Not everything here is good, Neel. Can't you see that? Baba works too hard and risks his life every time he goes into the reserve. Cyclones come and destroy our crops. In the city, girls can study as much as boys and work at all kinds of jobs. I wish *all* of us could live there."

"I wish you could take the exam instead of me."

"Ha! Our school has never sent a girl to compete for the scholarship." It was true. This was partly because many of the island girls never made it to Class Five—they were sent to the city to earn money for their families or pulled out of school to work at home like Rupa. Neel's sister got up early to pump and haul water, feed the animals, make patties out of cow dung for fuel, wash clothes, tend the garden, cook, and clean. Now she took the empty pot outside to wash it at the pump.

Ma was still chanting in a low voice behind the sari, and it was harder than ever for Neel to concentrate, especially on geometry. Proofs tied his brain into knots as tight as the ones on his father's fishing nets. Problems about triangles, rectangles, and circles didn't make any sense, no matter how much he squinted at or angled the page. His fingers, unlike Baba's, were clumsy around tools, especially ones as delicate as a protractor, compass, or ruler. Plus he kept worrying about the cub. Where was she hiding? Who would find her first? If only he could tell the rangers about Gupta's plan! They came down hard on poachers in the Sunderbans. *How dare he even think about stealing one of our cubs! I'd like to cut up* his *body parts and sell them on the black market.*

Rupa's next indoor task was to sift through a bag of uncooked rice from the market and pick out the small stones the vendors mixed in to make it weigh more.

Neel was tired of keeping his thoughts to himself. "That Gupta thinks he's so big! I can't stand him!"

His sister frowned. "I know. I wish Baba didn't have to work for him."

"At least Baba doesn't do any dirty work," Neel said, watching his sister pour more rice into the flat basket on her lap. He remembered Baba carving Gupta's balcony out of *sundari* wood, but he didn't say anything to his sister. *Let her find out for herself, or better yet, never find out.*

"Some people will do anything for money," Rupa said.

"You're right. Wait—isn't that why you all want me to go to school in Kolkata—for all the money I might earn in the future?"

"No—for the *opportunity*, crazy. Which reminds me: get to work. And I mean *study*—not daydream or doodle or write a poem like you usually do." Ruffling her brother's hair, Rupa took the sifted rice outside to wash it and put it on the stove.

After writing what he knew was the wrong answer to the first geometry problem, Neel put his pencil and protractor down and rested his head on his arms. It wasn't fair. All he wanted was to live at home, fish, build, carve, and hunt honey, like his father. But Baba wouldn't teach him those skills, and it was all because of Neel's success in school. Why had he been given this useless ability to absorb the meaning of words, sentences, stories, books? A boy didn't need to read or write well to become a fisherman or a carpenter.

After a while his sister came in again. Immediately Neel sat up, grabbed his compass, and started twisting it around on the page.

"I can see through the window, you know," Rupa scolded, stirring sugar into a hot, milky cup of tea for Neel. She always saved the tea bag from his morning tea to use it again in the afternoon. "You can't learn math while snoring."

"I wasn't snoring!"

Ma pushed back the sari to intervene. "Rupa! Go pump more water and peel the potatoes. And don't scold your brother—I'm sure he'll start studying harder than ever now."

"I was pouring his tea, Ma," Rupa said, but she grabbed the bucket and headed outside again.

Ma slowly followed, dropping a kiss on Neel's head and humming a song under her breath. Neel liked hearing his mother make music again—she had been sick for so long, her temperature raging until she hardly recognized them. The medicine to cure dysentery had been expensive, but it had done the job. She was still weak, but at least now she was able to walk outside in the sunshine and fresh air.

He sighed and turned the page. Maybe he could make sense of the algebra problems his teacher had assigned. Those were a bit more interesting than geometry, but he still had to push his brain harder than he liked. He could almost hear it groaning inside his head as he tried to concentrate. The problem was that math seemed so boring; his brain never needed urging when it came to reading or writing. He picked up his pencil and began to try to untangle an equation with unknown x's and unnamed y's.

six

BABA GOT BACK LATE. The moon had risen, and rice was simmering on the clay stove when Neel spotted him coming into the courtyard. Usually his father stopped to scratch the goats' heads and check their pen for water. They'd bleat in bliss, and the chickens and rooster would cluster around his feet as if they, too, welcomed him home. Only after greeting and caring for the animals did Baba wash his feet, legs, arms, and hands with the water in the bucket Rupa left for him. But today the bleating and clucking was in vain. Baba strode past the animals and went straight to the pump.

"Neel, come quickly and eat," Ma called from the courtyard.

Neel walked to the threshold and slipped into his sandals. Usually he ran to join Baba, but today his feet dragged. What would his father say about the encounter with Headmaster? Would he be angry?

But Baba didn't say a word. His face looked as grooved and gnarled as an old door. He stayed quiet as Rupa and Ma served lentils, rice, spinach, potatoes, and eggs. Usually he complimented the cooking, joked, and told stories about his day. But today he only spoke to turn down Ma's offer of a second egg, and Neel followed his example. Like the other women and older girls in the village, Ma and Rupa ate later, after the men and children, and Baba always made sure there was plenty left in the pots when he and Neel were done eating.

The meal was ending as silently as it had begun. Baba didn't even look at any of them. He ate with shoulders slumped, frowning at his plate.

"Baba . . . I'm sorry about today," Neel said finally, when he could no longer stand the silence. "I'll start studying harder—I promise."

"You heard Headmaster, Neel," Baba said. "Studying harder won't help."

"Why not?" Ma asked. "I can promise you the boy

studied all afternoon and evening. He will win that scholarship—I know he can do it!"

But Baba only sighed and shook his head. He stood up and trudged into the house, his figure as bent as if he were carrying a heavy load of wood on his strong shoulders.

That night Neel slept fitfully, waking from a nightmare about a pack of vultures tearing the cub's body to shreds. Had she been found? Was a boat carrying her to the port of Kolkata so she could be smuggled out of the country and sold? If she was still on the island, where could she be hiding? He couldn't fall back to sleep; he could barely keep his heart from racing like an out-of-control rickshaw. Taking a deep breath, he forced himself to practice a habit he'd invented to settle down after a bad dream. Bit by bit, his mind began to map out the island he knew so well, strolling from home to school, to the market, and around the other side, then detouring through the interior, circling ponds, crossing creeks, exploring forests. This time, however, he couldn't help taking the cub with him. He followed her mentally as she left the reserve, swam across the wide waterway, reached the island's shore, climbed up the bank, crossed the path, disappeared through the trees, and padded beside a twisting creek. Crocodiles lurked on the banks—could one have captured the cub in its powerful jaws? They often dragged away their prey before devouring it. His heart thumped faster instead of slower—the relaxing trick wasn't working this time. *Stay alive, baby. Your mother wants you home. That's where you belong—safe and sound on your island.* Finally he fell asleep from sheer exhaustion.

Baba was still shrouded in the same strange silence during breakfast, and this time Neel couldn't bring himself to try to break it. *A scolding or even a beating might be better than this*, he thought, longing for the easy chatter and laughter that usually accompanied their meals. Weary after his restless night, he dressed for school and trudged to the well to wait for Ajay.

A few women gathering water greeted him. "Our whole village is counting on you to win that scholarship," one said. "You will make your *ma* and *baba* so proud."

"I hope so, Auntie," said Neel, shifting his feet and watching for his friend. He was sure Ajay would have new details about the cub, since he and Viju lived near each other.

Ajay came bounding over, swinging his satchel.

"Did they find her?" Neel asked as soon as they were out of earshot of the women.

"Three of Gupta's men were out searching all night. Viju went with them, but there was no sign of the cub anywhere."

Neel exhaled in relief. "Thank goodness. We have to find her first, Ajay!"

"Not me. I don't want to get in trouble. Let's not talk about Gupta anymore—it's too dangerous."

It was hard to avoid the subject of the cub's escape at school. Again and again Teacher disciplined his Class Five students for discussing her chances of survival instead of doing their classwork. Only Ajay and Neel kept silent. Their classmates didn't realize the cub was facing something even more dangerous than crocodiles or hunger.

Just as the last bell rang, Headmaster stalked into their classroom. Immediately Teacher and all fifty of the students rose to their feet. "Good afternoon, Headmaster," they chorused.

Headmaster didn't return their greeting. "We need to talk," he said to Teacher.

"Class dismissed," Teacher said. He made sure the students were standing in a straight line as they waited to exit the room. Headmaster, however, adjusted the order, taking Neel by the arm and pulling him to the back. Ajay immediately joined his friend.

As the front of the line began filing out, the sound of marching muffled Teacher's words to Headmaster. Headmaster waited until only a few students were left in the room. His voice was as loud as the scolding of a rhesus monkey high in the *sundari* trees. "Stupid rich man fed me tea and gave me a rickshaw ride home. But would he donate any rupees to our school? No! All the furniture here is falling apart—including these ancient desks!"

Thwack! Headmaster kicked an old desk so hard one of the legs broke. The desk tipped to the side like a boat about to capsize, and a pile of books and papers tumbled to the floor. "Boys, pick those up immediately," he commanded, but Ajay and Neel had already started gathering the books. It wouldn't be right to leave them on the floor or step on them with dirty feet.

Teacher squatted by the tilting desk and tried to straighten the broken leg. "Looks as if it's beyond repair," he said, sighing.

"Think the boy has any chance at that scholarship?" Headmaster asked, tipping his head in Neel's direction.

Teacher stood up, giving up on the slanted desk. "I've been reviewing portions of last year's exam with him. As I told you, sir, he's doing exceptionally well in all the subjects but math."

"Let me see his last attempt."

Teacher rummaged through a file and pulled out Neel's assignment from the day before, which was covered with red ink. "With fifty students, sir, and my after-school tutoring, I can't spend much time helping him. I grade his practice exams and assign him extra problems every day, but he doesn't seem to be mastering it."

They were discussing him as though he weren't there, but that didn't surprise Neel. Elders had the right to do this. His face burned as Headmaster scanned the page.

"I could do these problems in my sleep, and *I* studied them forty-five years ago. There are so many careless mistakes! He's not even trying, is he?" Headmaster crumpled the paper and tossed it on the ground.

"Neel *is* by far the brightest child in the school, sir," Teacher said. "You've always picked the top-scoring student to represent our school."

"Yes, but this particular one doesn't understand the

gift of a good education." Headmaster threw a scowl at Neel, who averted his eyes and went back to gathering papers. "He needs expert help at this point. That tutor from Kolkata might be able to get him in shape—I hear he can actually make the laziest student *want* to learn. But this one's father is too poor to afford his fees."

Neel's fist tightened around his crumpled math homework. Headmaster might have the right to talk about Neel's failures, but how dare he drag Baba's name through the mud?

Teacher seemed to agree with Neel's silent defense. "His father's a good worker, sir. The whole island's been struggling since the cyclone."

"That's why the boy needs to seize this opportunity with both hands," said Headmaster. He sighed. "Well, as the Americans like to say, 'You can only make a horse drink so much water.'"

You can lead a horse to water, but you can't make it drink, Neel corrected, biting his lip so his anger wouldn't make him say it aloud. Teacher's English skills were better than Headmaster's, but Neel noticed he didn't correct the mangled phrase either.

Headmaster switched back to Bangla, swinging his

hand wrist-down at the boys. "You two good-for-nothings are dismissed," he said, brushing by them and stalking out of the classroom.

Slowly Neel unclenched his fist, just as Baba had done the day before, and his homework dropped into the waste bin. He didn't want to see those problems again, covered with red marks. What a lot of time he'd wasted the night before! He could have been in the mangrove forest instead, looking for the cub.

Another student came in and took a seat. He was one of the few boys on the island whose parents paid Teacher for extra tutoring after school.

"Here's tonight's math," Teacher said, handing Neel a sheaf of papers. "Do the best you can."

As Neel and Ajay walked home, Neel imagined a detailed scene of the mother tiger leaping through the school window and pouncing on Headmaster. She could track Gupta down and devour him next.

Ajay turned to Neel. "You don't have a chance at that scholarship, do you?"

"Not a hope in a million."

"I'm glad. You'd have to study in Kolkata for years, and then you'd probably get a job there, or somewhere else far away."

"I know. Horrible thought." As they walked the familiar path, Neel stopped every now and then to peer through the underbrush. "I'd like to search the trees behind the freshwater pond. It's hard to find the trail that leads to the hiding places back there. I don't think Viju could do it without me."

"Be quiet, will you?" Ajay kept his own voice low. "No use looking in the daytime anyway. She's probably fast asleep somewhere deep in the forest. Gupta's men are going to search again tonight, Viju said. That's when tigers roam about."

"They'll be sure to catch her, then," said Neel, with another pang for the cub. "It's going to be a full moon in a few days."

"Maybe she'll swim back to the reserve," Ajay whispered hopefully.

"Maybe." But Neel guessed the cub would be too terrified to venture out of her hiding place, except maybe to scavenge for food. He was sure she had found a spot where there was no human scent and was staying there until her mother came for her.

They'd reached the pond. "Speaking of a swim . . . ," Ajay said.

Neel hesitated. He pictured the new pages of math

in his satchel, which meant hours at his desk late into the night. A quick swim could refresh his tired mind and body. *Besides, I'm sure Headmaster won't walk this way two days in a row.* "I'll beat you this time, Ajay!"

The two boys moved so quickly, it seemed that their discarded clothes were still floating to the ground as their bodies hit the water. With a shout Neel grabbed Ajay's heel, yanked his friend backward, and headed across the pond as fast as he could. Ajay passed him easily in a minute, laughing as he swam by.

seven

THREE LONG DAYS and nights passed without any sign of the cub. The air on the island was thick with talk and tension. Was she still alive? Would she ever be found? Meanwhile the rangers were frantically trying to calm the mother tiger and keep her safely inside the reserve. The fence was strong, but it always needed repair, and an angry tiger could claw open a small tear in no time. If the mother tiger escaped and swam to their island, she could kill several people before the rangers could tranquilize her.

Ma was praying more than usual, and Baba still wasn't speaking much. He returned from work late and barely ate, sitting in that same strange, troubled gloom. For the first time in his life, Neel, too, was finding it difficult to eat. Had Headmaster's public scolding broken Baba's heart?

"Baba," Neel said on the third evening, ending the heavy silence, "I was wondering something."

Baba roused himself. "Yes, Neel. What is it?"

"That cub. Don't you think that you and I could find her—"

"Too dangerous, Neel. This island's not as safe as it used to be."

"But I—"

"Listen to your *baba*, Neel," Ma added. "Stay close to home. And study. That's your task."

And that was the end of that. That night, knowing Gupta's men were out hunting, Neel tossed and turned, his brain taking him on imaginary searches for the cub. It was a full moon, so the whole island would be illuminated with light except for the most dense corners of the mangrove forest. As he worried over the cub, he could hear his parents talking on the other side of the divider. Even though they kept their voices low, he caught snippets of their whispered conversation.

"You're already working so hard to pay back the doctor," Ma said. "What more can you do?"

"I *must* earn some extra money. Our boy is the smartest in all the Sunderbans. He could become a big man, an educated man, like Headmaster."

You're bigger than he is, Baba, Neel thought.

Ma said it for him: "That man is not better than you—everybody in this village respects Neel's father."

"But I'm losing our boy's chance to win that scholarship!" Baba sounded both angry and sad.

Neel's stomach tightened around the small amount of rice he'd managed to swallow. It wasn't Baba's fault that Neel was going to lose the scholarship. *If only Headmaster hadn't chosen me to represent the school!* Why couldn't his best friend have inherited a school-smart brain from *his* father, the teacher? Then maybe Ajay could have been the one chosen to take the exam.

The following night, he was woken by the urgency in Baba's voice. "He won't be able to win without that special tutor, and I can't afford to hire him! There's no other way."

"Shhh," Ma said. "You'll find another way, Husband. You always do."

"If only—if only it wasn't so hard for me to earn extra money."

Baba's voice broke as he said this, and Neel brushed

the back of his hand across his eyes. Hard. This was all his fault. He squirmed on his mat, wishing uselessly that Headmaster hadn't selected him, picturing the cub chased by a hungry crocodile, counting the minutes until the sun would finally rise. Why was it taking so long?

Two days later, Baba arrived home long after dark. The waning, still-bright moon had risen high in the night sky by the time they ate. Tonight's *rui* fish was spiced with black pepper and turmeric, and Ma had made her tasty cauliflower and potato curry. It was good to eat her cooking again, but Baba didn't compliment it. Again he ate hunched over his food, tense and quiet, paying no attention to anything except what was going on inside his own head.

After dinner, as Neel waited for his sister to wash the plates, they heard their parents arguing inside the hut. Without a word Neel and Rupa crept to the threshold to listen. Baba's voice was low, but they could hear it clearly: "What else can I do? Gupta asked me again to join the hunt. He's doubled the pay. I'll go after the children are asleep."

The metal *thali* Rupa was clutching clattered on the stone. Neel rushed into the hut, followed closely by his sister. For once they didn't bother to take off

their sandals before entering the hut and running to
their father.

"No, Baba!"

"*Chup!*" Ma sternly scolded them to be quiet, but
they didn't obey.

"Is Gupta hunting the cub tonight, Baba?" Rupa
demanded. "What does he want with her?"

"You know what he wants!" Neel shouted. "To sell
her on the black market! You can't do this, Baba!"

"You may neither command nor contradict your
father," scolded Ma. "Lower your voice this minute,
Neel. And both of you, take off your sandals. It's hard
enough to keep this hut clean without the two of you
dragging mud and dirt in here."

Neel swallowed hard. He and Rupa headed back
to the threshold and yanked off their sandals. Then
they both marched back to their father, who was
standing where they had left him, head bowed, hands
hanging limply.

"How can you think of handing the cub to a man
like Gupta, Baba?" Rupa asked, her voice shaky.

Baba didn't lift his head to meet her eyes, and there
was a long silence. "I don't see what else to do," he said
finally. "Neel needs that tutor. This is the only chance

I have to earn the extra money. Gupta's only hiring two or three men."

"I *don't* need a tutor, Baba," Neel said. Now *his* voice was shaky, and tears were blurring his vision. "Please. I can study on my own."

"You heard Headmaster," Baba said. "You won't improve without a tutor. I'm your father. I must do what I can to help you."

"I don't even want to take that stupid exam! Or win that scholarship!" Neel wiped his eyes furiously with his sleeve. *Enough with the tears! You're in Class Five, almost Class Six! Grow up, Neel!*

"So Headmaster was right?" Ma asked incredulously. "You *aren't* trying? Are you crazy, Neel?"

Baba straightened as though Neel's words had given him new resolve. "You see? He doesn't understand what a chance this is for him. That's why he needs this tutor."

Neel looked at Rupa for help, but she shot him one of her "I told you so" looks. He took a deep breath to try to stop the tears. "I don't want to leave home, Baba."

"Ay-yo!" Ma exclaimed. "What are you thinking, Son? You don't want to leave *here*?"

"I want to stay with you, Baba," said Neel. "That's all I've ever wanted. I'll take care of our land like you do. Our rice and peppers came back so fast after the cyclone! And we've never gone hungry, Baba. Never! You're a much bigger man than that Gupta, Baba! *Or* Headmaster."

"But they can both read. And write. And that gives them a certain kind of power in this world, Neel—don't you see? I want *you* to have that power. Besides, we have different talents, you and I. This is mine." Baba lifted his hand and showed Neel his palm. Then his big hand rested on Neel's head. "And this is yours."

Rupa was mopping her cheeks with the end of her sari. "Neel's brain isn't worth you handing a baby tiger to Gupta—"

Baba put his other hand on Rupa's shoulder. His face looked tired and old. "I've made my decision. No more discussion. We probably won't find the poor creature anyway, and this fuss will be for nothing. But I'll get paid regardless. And we must keep Gupta's search a secret. Don't tell a soul. Daughter, bring my mask, will you? And one of the flashlights."

"Yes, Baba," Rupa managed to say through her tears. She turned to obey.

"Husband, you're not going into the reserve, are you?" Ma asked, alarm in her voice. Baba wore only his mask when he ventured behind the fence, even though lately it seemed like the decoys didn't fool the tigers anymore. Two of the fishermen who'd been killed this year had been wearing them.

"There's a chance that the mother tiger broke loose and came across the river," Baba said. "The mask might distract her, at least."

Rupa handed him the plastic decoy mask, and Baba slipped it on so that the painted human face covered the back of his head.

"I'll be back before dawn," he said. Picking up a flashlight and one of the sturdy *sundari* sticks from the pile in the corner, he left the hut.

eight

HEADING STRAIGHT FOR Bon Bibi's shrine, Ma began to light incense and chant prayers. Slowly Rupa went back outside to finish the dishes, and Neel followed. He squatted by the pump, shaky and sick. It felt like another cyclone had hit the island, turning the soil to water underneath his feet.

"I can't believe it," he said. "I just can't believe it."

Rupa was scrubbing a *thali* furiously. "Protect the tigers. Plant trees. That's always what he taught us." She looked up at the tall *sundari* trees silhouetted against the moon and wiped her cheeks again.

Neel couldn't bring himself to be angry at Baba. "This is all Headmaster's fault, choosing me to take that exam. I hate that man almost as much as I hate studying!"

Rupa shot him a sharp look. "Do you really hate it? But what about all those books you read? And the stories you're always scribbling?"

Neel didn't answer. That was one thing about Rupa—he could never fool her the way he could everyone else. He was quiet, watching her dry and stack the *thalis*. The *sundari* trees swayed in the wind. It was almost as if they were beckoning. He thought of the cub hiding somewhere nearby, far from her mother, scared and lonely. Gupta's fat face flashed in front of his eyes. "We should at least *try* to save her, Didi," he said. "I can't stand the thought of her falling into that awful man's hands."

"We should try to save *Baba*," Rupa said. "He'll never forgive himself if he's the one who finds her. But what can we do?"

Neel thought of their father's grim face. "We can look for that cub ourselves. You and me. Tonight."

"What makes you think we'll find her? Gupta's men have searched everywhere by now."

"There might be a place or two that they don't know about."

"Do you really think so?" Rupa asked.

"Viju was right—I know this island better than anybody, Didi. Besides, they haven't found her yet, have they?"

Rupa was quiet for a second, and then she slammed the last dry *thali* on top of the pile. "OK, then. We'll try to find her. But what happens if we do?"

"The ranger told me she'd come to us if we lured her with milk. It might take a while for her to trust us." Now it was Neel's turn to sound doubtful. "Even if we do find her and she comes to us, how will we carry her to the reserve without anyone seeing us?"

"First things first," Rupa said. "If you were a tiger cub, far from your mother, where would *you* hide? Go inside and think hard, Neel. Use every bit of that smart brain of yours. Meanwhile I'll finish cleaning up. We'll head out once Ma is lying down."

Their mother prayed for a long time that night. Neel perched on his chair and waited for her to stop chanting. Where could that cub be hiding? Suddenly he remembered the nightmare that had woken him, and how he had tried to steady himself by mapping the island in his head. He'd tracked the cub mentally. Why couldn't he do that on paper? With a jolt of energy, Neel took out a piece of graph paper and a sharp pencil. Then he pulled out the protractor, ruler, and compass. *Might as well do this right*, he thought. *Each millimeter is one hundred steps, Neel.* He grinned for the first time in days, realizing he sounded just like Headmaster mangling a saying.

Ma finished her prayers and came in to say good night. "Studying in earnest this time? That's my smart boy. I've always known that you would find a way to help our family."

Rupa returned from her chores and studied Neel's drawing. She turned to their mother. "You should rest, Ma. Remember what the doctor said."

"Come and lie beside me, Daughter," Ma said. "If you stroke my forehead, maybe I can fall asleep. And wake me the moment your *baba* returns."

Rupa gave her brother an encouraging pat on the shoulder before following Ma behind the sari. Neel continued to draw. He had to map it perfectly, step by step, centimeter by centimeter, this terrain that his feet knew so well: town center on the far side of the island, school building near the market and police station, the long walk past a dense mangrove forest, the detour to the freshwater pond, four creeks that crossed the raised path curving around this side of the island, his family's small parcel of land, the tall tamarind tree, the dock where his father's *nauka* floated with the others . . . He bent over the paper, measuring distances with the ruler, erasing and redrawing the curves of the shore and the width of the creeks and deltas, twisting the compass to draw the circle of the pond, and using the protractor to angle the twists of the path.

As he began to sketch the patches of dense forest in the interior of the island, he thought of the times he'd played hide-and-seek with Ajay and Viju. Where did they hide? He remembered squeezing through the guava trees and dense bushes on the far side of the pond, crawling on his hands and knees in the underbrush that bordered the rice paddies, ducking behind the long, arched bridge spanning the widest part of the creek . . . Now his drawing was taking him to places Gupta's men might never think to look. Thanks to the thick bushes and the swamps and muddy banks that bordered the creeks, only small bodies could wiggle into the dry nooks and crannies of the island. *She's got to be in one of these spots!* he thought, beginning to calculate the high tide for the night. It had been a full moon three nights earlier, so if the high tides came in at

1:30 a.m. and 1:30 p.m. that day, the next day they would have come in forty-five minutes later, at 2:15 a.m. and 2:15 p.m., and so on. *That means tonight's high tide will come at 3:45 a.m.—we'll need to start searching soon!*

Neel turned off the lamp and heard his sister's sari rustle as she eased through the divider to join him. She was carrying the extra flashlight and two tiger masks.

"I finished my map," Neel said, his voice low as he spread it out.

"Good. I knew your head would come to the rescue. Let me see it."

Rupa flashed the light across it and smiled. "Looks like you used some math, didn't you?"

He shrugged. "I had to. I needed it to be as true to scale as possible. I thought of three or four good hiding spots as I was sketching—places Gupta's men would never think to look. Not even Baba."

"Really? That's wonderful, Neel!"

"There's one behind the pond. We'll start with that. We need to leave now so we don't run into the high tide."

"OK. Let's go." Rupa handed Neel a mask and the flashlight. Then she slipped a decoy over the back of her own head and picked up the empty pail and a cotton undervest of Neel's.

"Bring a *sundari* stick," she whispered.

He grabbed one from the pile in the corner and followed Rupa outside to the courtyard. Slowly, so the gate wouldn't creak, she opened the goat pen and stroked the mother goat's back. The goat seemed surprised to see visitors this late, but she relaxed at Rupa's familiar touch.

After a few more soothing words and caresses, Rupa was able to milk her until the pail was more than half full. "Let's go," she whispered, tucking the vest into the waist of her sari. "Bring the stick. And don't use that flashlight unless we absolutely need it. We'd be spotted right away."

nine

As they hurried along the familiar path to the pond, Neel was glad the moonlight made it bright enough to see without the flashlight. But it also meant Gupta's men could spot them at any minute. *And Baba, our Baba, is with them!*

"Maybe they're searching on the other side of the island," Rupa whispered. Clearly she, too, was worried about being caught.

Now they were almost to the detour that led to the pond. In the moonlight Neel was able to push through the bushes and find the thin trail that circled the water. He'd walked there in the daylight and his feet knew the way, but the sounds were different now. Snakes slithered freely at night, and a cobra bite could be deadly. Neel trod carefully and kept the light on the ground around their feet. Rupa stayed close behind him, and he could hear the milk sloshing in the pail. Was it too loud?

On the other side of the pond, guava trees crowded the bank. When the trail faded into dense foliage, Neel handed Rupa the flashlight. "I'm going to hunt around a bit," he whispered. "She might be in there. Keep the light on me if you can."

"Be careful—don't go too far."

As Neel crawled around the tree trunks and through the bushes, Rupa followed his movements with the flashlight. But there was no sign of the cub— no sound of mewing and no pugmarks anywhere. After more fruitless searching, they headed back to the main path.

"Where next?" Rupa asked.

About an hour had passed since they'd left the house, Neel guessed. He pulled out his map, and once again Rupa shone the light across it. "It's still low tide," he said. "We can search the banks by the big creek."

Deep in a ravine carved by the water at the southern tip of the island, past the reach of the tides and through a tunnel of prickly bushes, there was a narrow cave in the big creek's bank. The place was cool and dry and completely out of sight. He'd found it while playing hide-and-seek with Ajay and Viju years before. His friends had been searching for him on the bridge, and he'd stayed hidden for a while before creeping out and startling them with a whoop. He'd never told them about the cave and had forgotten about it himself until his map had taken him back to it. He doubted anybody else in the village knew it was there. *Might have been washed away by the cyclone*, Neel thought, *but it's worth a try.*

This creek was so big it was almost a river. A long, high bamboo bridge spanned it, and dense, prickly foliage grew up the high, steep banks on either side. The only way down was during low tide, when a muddy path near one end of the bridge led to the estuary shore. As the high tide came in, salty water covered the lower half of the path and the shore and coursed deep into the ravine.

Neel had calculated the tides perfectly; the whole path was above water. Moonlight sparkled across the wide, wet shore. Fiddler crabs scuttled here and there, excavating mud to create burrows before the tide came in. Reaching out a hand to help his sister jump down to the bank, Neel again kept an eye out for cobras. Maybe the bright moonlight here would keep them away. Other creatures, however, hunted for prey both day and night—like crocodiles. He risked a sweep of the bank with the flashlight.

"Footprints!" Rupa hissed, pointing.

Men had been searching along the banks and under the bridge. "These were made after the last high tide," Neel said, wondering if any belonged to Baba. "They're still fresh."

"Turn off the light," Rupa said quickly. "Anyone passing on the bridge can see it."

Neel switched it off after making sure a long, still log nearby didn't have teeth and eyes. He led his sister deeper into the ravine. The strip of mud between the water and the bank narrowed, even though it was still low tide. Suddenly a big cluster of *golpata* trees jogged his memory. He put down the *sundari* stick and motioned to Rupa to join him.

She set the pail of milk down carefully and gazed up at the bank behind the *golpata* trees. It rose steeply and was covered by prickly bushes, vines, and bracken. "I don't see how the cub could hide anywhere around here."

"There's a perfect hiding spot in here. Unless it got washed away."

Neel pushed apart the tall, wide *golpata* fronds. With a quick glance to make sure the bridge, path, and shore were still deserted, he switched the light on again and angled it against the bank. There it was! The entrance to a long, low open space that twisted through the foliage and led deep into the bank. The tunnel-like space was narrowed by many more roots and branches than the last time he'd been here, but it was still visible.

"We have to crawl in there?" Rupa asked.

"I'll go first."

Using the *golpata* branches for leverage, Neel hoisted himself into the open space. Thorns and roots clawed at him from the sides and above his head, tearing at his hair, skin, and the decoy mask still attached to the back of his head. The front of his body was covered with mud, but he managed to slither forward. *Used to be more like a tunnel through this bank*, he thought. *Now it's barely passable.* Rupa climbed up behind him, and he could hear her mutter as her sari caught on the thorns. He wondered if her arms were getting as scratched as his.

The space narrowed even more as it cut deeper into the bank. The soil was dry now, completely out of reach of the water, except perhaps for when a tidal bore—a dangerous surge of water—rose suddenly after a storm and flooded the creek.

Neel kept kneeing and elbowing his way forward, steadying the flashlight as he pushed away branches and roots. "Look!" he called suddenly, aiming the light at a patch of soil just in front of him.

He leaned aside so Rupa could see, and heard the sharp intake of his sister's breath. It was a tiny pugmark. And then another. There may have been others on the bank and in the space behind them, but they would have washed away with the ebb and flow of the tide.

Carefully Neel inched forward. If he was remembering correctly, they were almost to the cave carved deep into the muddy bank. Pushing through the last thorny bush that obstructed his way, Neel shone the light into the hollow.

He gasped.

White and black and orange-gold fur.

Glowing, round eyes rimmed with black.

She was there.

ten

THE CUB WAS ON HER FEET, her back to the bank, staring unblinkingly into the flashlight. Her legs were short, her belly low to the ground. Two round ears, edged with white fur, twitched forward. Her golden nose quivered, tipped by a semicircle of black fur and two angled nostrils. Thin, white whiskers shimmered in the light, and a pink tongue poked out from above her white chin. A dazzling pattern of small black stripes was etched across her white-and-golden fur. Shrimp and crab shells were littered around the floor of the small cave. She must have ventured out to hunt during low tide and brought her prey back to eat in safety.

Rupa crawled forward as far as she could, leaning across her brother's back. "It's her," she breathed. "It's really her."

They gazed at the beautiful creature for a long minute, and then Neel switched off the flashlight. Although the cub seemed startled, she didn't look scared. But he couldn't reach her with his hands; she was backed deep inside the cave, and his body wouldn't fit beyond this spot as it had when he was younger. How could they lure her out?

"Will she come to us?" Rupa whispered.

"I don't think so," he whispered back, "but let's see."

"Try to sound like a mother tiger."

"What? I don't know how."

"Do the best you can."

There wasn't enough room in the opening to turn around, so the two of them backed out feetfirst. Neel had never heard tigers firsthand, only people who had imitated them, but he tried calling to the cub with a low chuffing noise. Stopping for a minute, he strained to hear any movement from the cave, but no sound came.

"Keep going," he whispered to Rupa, who had also stopped to listen.

They crawled back a bit farther, and Neel tried mewing, but that didn't work either. The cub didn't budge. He tried a combination of whimpering, mewing, and chuffing, stopping every now and then to listen. Complete silence from the cub—it was almost as if she were holding her breath until they left her alone.

"We need to bring back some milk," he said finally, giving up. "Let's go."

Once they were back on the bank, Rupa smiled at her brother. "You found her, Neel. Nice work. But you certainly don't speak tiger."

"I'd like to hear you try it." Neel glanced up at the bridge nervously. Still no one in sight, and no sound of footsteps. "What's your plan to lure her out of there?"

Neel's vest was still tucked into the waist of Rupa's sari, and she yanked it out. Stooping, she dunked the vest in the pail of milk, soaked it for a minute, and then wrung it out loosely. "Let me go first this time. Bring the stick." She wrapped the end of her sari around the milky vest. Then she draped the bundle across her back to keep it from getting muddy and hoisted herself into the tunnel again.

Crawling through the thorny passageway was easier this time because their bodies had broken a wider path. Neel slid the long stick up to his sister when they reached the hollow and shone the flashlight on her hands. Rupa managed to tie the milky vest to the end of the stick and then carefully pushed it deeper into the hollow until it was within the cub's reach. Neel held his breath as his sister mewed, waited, mewed, and waited again. He had to admit that Rupa's tiger imitation sounded better than his.

Rupa's body was blocking most of his view, but to Neel's amazement, he heard an answering mew, and then a soft sucking sound. The cub was drinking the milk from the vest! After a while, centimeter by centimeter, Rupa began to pull the stick out of the cave. Neel backed down to make room. But as soon as they moved, the sucking sound stopped.

"Isn't she coming?" Neel asked anxiously.

"No! She's staying against the back of the cave."

Once again Rupa crawled forward and pushed the stick deep into the cave, offering the milky vest to the baby. The sucking began and kept going—the cub was obviously hungry—but stopped as soon as they moved backward. They tried the trick a third time, but still the cub wouldn't come toward them. It was getting late; Neel wasn't sure exactly how long they'd been in the tunnel, but the tide was probably already swelling the creek.

"We've got to get out," he told his sister after she'd tried for a fourth time and failed again. "But we can't leave her here."

"I don't know what else to do. She's not coming. I'll leave the vest so she gets used to our scent, and we'll come back tomorrow."

Quickly Rupa untied the vest from the stick and shoved it forward toward the cub. Neel was already backing down the passageway as fast as he could. His sister's feet were keeping pace in front of him, but as they pushed through the *golpata* fronds, he gulped. The tide was even higher than he had anticipated. The pail was floating instead of standing, and they were going to have to wade through knee-high water to return to the shore.

Rupa grabbed the pail. They sloshed under the bridge to the shore. Neel didn't bother to rub out their footprints as they climbed the lower half of the trail that sloped up the bank. The creek was rising fast, and any traces of their trek would be underwater soon. He did take the time to smear the mud on the upper part of the trail while his sister waited by the bridge.

"If only she had come out," Neel said when he joined Rupa.

"She's been safe there for days. At least we know she's alive."

He frowned. "For now, yes. But they might find her before we get the news to the rangers."

"I know, but we can't do anything more tonight."

Dripping with salty water and covered with mud, they jogged home as fast as they could. Neel braced himself for the sound of footsteps, followed by a shout and then a chase. But Gupta's men must indeed have been searching the other side of the island. There was neither sight nor sound of them.

"We'll have to hide our dirty clothes," Rupa whispered as they entered the quiet courtyard. Even the goats were asleep. "I'll wash them tomorrow."

Baba wasn't back yet. Rupa and Neel took turns at the pump, washing themselves off and changing into clean clothes. As his sister put away the stick, pail, and masks, Neel crawled wearily onto his mat. Just as he slipped into sleep, a rooster crowed. His last thought was of the cub, curled into the cave with his milky vest tucked beside her. He and Rupa had to get their news to the rangers before she was discovered.

eleven

WHEN RUPA GREETED Neel after school the next day, he tossed his satchel in the corner of the hut and left it there. He wasn't even going to pretend to study. How could anyone concentrate on geometry or algebra after seeing the beautiful face of that cub?

Ma wasn't feeling quite as well today, so she was resting on her mat, and Baba was nowhere in sight. Neel helped Rupa finish her chores so they had time to sit in the shade of the *sundari* trees and hatch their next plan.

"We have to tell the rangers we found her," Rupa said, her voice low. "But how do we get to the reserve?"

Baba had always used his *nauka* to ferry them from

island to island. *For the first time ever, we can't ask him for transportation*, Neel thought, but like his sister, he didn't say it aloud. "Maybe we can borrow a *nauka*," he said instead.

They ran through their list of relatives, but anyone in their extended family would wonder why they weren't using Baba's *nauka*. Besides, they'd ask questions, and Neel and Rupa didn't want to tell anybody the truth. If their own father was going to hand the cub to Gupta, whom could they trust?

"I know!" Rupa cried. "We'll borrow a cell phone and ring up the rangers."

"Borrow a phone? From whom? Nobody's going to let us make a call in private."

"What about Ajay?" Rupa asked. "He can keep a secret."

"Ajay's father doesn't own a *nauka* or a phone. He gets paid a teacher's salary, remember?" Neel groaned. "And maybe he'd tell Gupta about the cub, too."

They sat in silence for a few minutes.

"Can't take the ferry," Rupa said sadly. "We'd have to ask Baba for the fare."

Now that they couldn't count on their father's help, their whole world felt washed away.

A light rain began to fall, and Rupa scurried to gather the dry clothes.

Neel ran to help, looking up at the sky. "Is it going to storm?"

"I hope not," Rupa said. "Anyway, it's not the season for cyclones."

"The weather's been so strange lately. And if a *ban* comes in . . ."

Neel didn't finish his sentence. The cub had managed to swim across the channel in low tide, but a surge of high water could reach the cave and drown her. If a *ban* were on the way, they'd hear shouts from all sides: "*Ban! Ban!* Tidal bore coming! Run for higher ground!" Could Neel and Rupa get to the cub before a big wave? *I'd have to try*, Neel thought. He pictured the cub's golden eyes, trembling nose, and patterned fur. She was so far from her mother! And so alone! He couldn't let a wave devour her, any more than he could let her be sold on the black market.

Rupa was following his thoughts. "At least let's get her out of that cave," she said. "Maybe we can hide her somewhere else until we get word to the rangers."

"But where? She found the best hiding spot on the island all on her own."

"Safe from people, maybe. But not from a *ban*. And the rain's getting worse."

Neel took a deep breath. "We have to get her out tonight and take her to the reserve in Baba's *nauka*. Without asking him."

"Is that right? Isn't that like lying to him?"

"Well, what did we do last night, then?"

Rupa didn't answer. There was nothing more to say. Saving the cub was the right thing—all Neel had to do was remember the cub's markings, small paws, and shining whiskers. *Baba, when you see her, you'll understand! You'll act like yourself again!*

When dinnertime came, the rain was pouring. Baba returned, dried off, and sat down to eat. He didn't wait for questions. "No sign of her," he said gruffly as Rupa piled rice on his *thali*. "But I got paid for last night. Two more nights and we'll have enough to pay for one tutoring session."

Rupa and Neel carefully avoided looking at each other. If all went according to their plan, there would be only one more night of cub hunting. For all of them. They had to get that cub to safety tonight!

twelve

AFTER DINNER the rain slowed, and Baba left without a word. Once Ma was asleep, Rupa and Neel armed themselves with the decoy masks, a flashlight, the long *sundari* stick, another unwashed shirt of Neel's, and a pail of fresh milk, covered this time to protect it from the rain. Again they timed their arrival at the creek for when the tide would be low. The path around the island was slippery, but their feet were used to walking in mud. The rain made it harder to hear any sounds of pursuit, but at least the lack of moonlight would make them harder to spot.

They clambered down to the shore, made their way under the bridge, and reached the *golpata* trees without having to wade in the water. Rupa readied the milky shirt, dipping it in the pail three times.

"Bend over," she said.

"Why?"

"You're smaller than me," she said. "If the cub comes toward you, you might be able to grab her."

"Not much smaller," Neel protested, but he obeyed his sister and felt her attaching the lure to his back.

"Keep still. Stay down."

"What? Why? Hey!"

Rupa had lifted his decoy mask and poured milk across his shoulders and neck. It was dripping down his back and into his shorts. He straightened with a jolt, and some of it trickled into his shirt, which was already wet from rain.

She spread the last bit of milk on the top of his head and across his shirt. "Squeeze the milk into the cloth," she said.

He did it quickly. The rain had stopped, and moonlight was breaking through the clouds. "Let's go."

As they pushed their way out through the *golpata* trees, Neel froze. Loud footsteps were clattering across the bridge. He pulled his sister behind the fronds, his heart pounding.

"What's that?" a voice called from above, carrying across the ravine. It was Viju!

Neel heard his sister's sharp intake of breath. She grabbed his hand.

"Where?"

"I see them! There, on the shore! Footprints." Viju's father!

"Those are our footprints. We searched there earlier, remember?" That was Baba's voice!

Rupa's hand clutched Neel's tightly. Would Baba and his companions come down to the creek? They'd left the pail on the bank. Would the men spot it?

But gradually the voices merged into a low rumble and faded into the distance. Neel heard his sister exhale and felt her hand trembling in his before she let go. He couldn't believe they were cowering from their own father—Baba, who had never lifted a hand against either of them! A wave of anger swept through him like a tidal bore. Gupta would never get that cub—not if he could help it! Squaring his shoulders, he turned and led the way into the underbrush. Would the cub still be there? Would she still be alive?

When they reached the entrance to the cave, Neel shone the light inside the hollow while his sister peered around his shoulder. A pair of startled eyes stared back at them. She was there! If only they could get her out this time!

The vest they'd left behind the night before was torn and dirty. When Neel extended the new lure, tied to the end of the *sundari* stick, the cub sucked hungrily at the milk-drenched shirt. After a short while, Neel motioned to Rupa to back out, but the cub didn't follow. They went through the routine again. And again. But the cub stayed at the back of the cave, sucking the milk only when the shirt came close to her.

"Tide's rising," Rupa hissed. "We have to get her out!"

Neel thought hard. Then he handed his sister the flashlight, put his hand on the milky shirt, and pushed it as far forward as he could. Wedging his shoulders inside the entrance to the cave, he used his feet to propel his hand and the shirt as deep into the cave as he could. He stretched both toward the cub. *Come on, little girl, here I am. I won't hurt you!*

There was a silence. Neel's body was blocking most of the light from the flashlight, so he couldn't see anything. But then he heard the soft pad of paws and the sounds of sucking and—he could hardly believe it— felt a rough little tongue licking the milk off his knuckles. He kept his hand as still as he could. *You know this smell, little one. It was on the shirt that stayed with you all night. Come on!*

Bit by bit, he moved his hand back. The soft sounds of licking and padding paws didn't stop. Soon, in the dim light that filtered in around his body, he glimpsed the tips of white whiskers. Next came a nose, just inches from his. And then a tongue, tasting his arm, his shoulders, and then—his cheek! Carefully, slowly, while the cub sucked the milk from his chin, Neel wrapped his arms around the tiny body. Gently he pulled her out of the cave into the tunnel.

His sister gasped. "Neel, she's so beautiful!"

Neel forgot for a moment about Baba and Gupta's men as he held the cub close. She nuzzled against him, still licking and pawing him. She wasn't much heavier than a baby goat, and her face was so sweet that he kissed it.

"Let's go, Neel," Rupa said softly.

As they backed out of the tunnel, Neel realized that the hardest part was still ahead. Somehow they had to get the cub to Baba's *nauka* without anyone catching them. And then row her to the reserve. It was going to take a miracle.

thirteen

WHEN THEY REACHED the bank, the tide was already ankle-high. Moonlight shimmered across the creek. Carefully Rupa moved closer to Neel and reached out to stroke the tiny animal. The cub licked her hands, and she chuckled in delight. "She knows me!"

"Shhh," Neel warned. "We're not out of danger yet."

Rupa's hand smoothed the orange-and-black fur. "What now?"

How would they make it to the dock? And if they did get caught, how would they explain themselves to Baba? The last thing Neel wanted was to dishonor their father, and he knew his sister felt the same way. He rubbed his cheek against the cub's soft head. *Getting her to safety is the best way we can respect everything that Baba taught us. Surely he would see that?*

"We'll have to make a run for it. Once we get to the boat, you can hold her while I row us to the reserve."

Rupa picked up the pail, flashlight, and stick. "OK. Let's go."

They waded through the water and climbed back onto the path, with Neel still cradling the cub. The island was quiet, but a dog barked in the distance as they jogged along the path, single file. Another dog joined in.

"Go faster, Neel," Rupa said urgently.

"I'm afraid I'll drop her."

When they reached the well, they heard the noise they'd been dreading.

Voices.

Men's voices.

Coming closer.

Moving fast.

"Stop!"

"Who's there?"

Now they had to run. Clutching the cub, Neel picked up his pace, Rupa at his heels. He threw a quick look over his shoulder. Lights bobbed on the path behind them as their pursuers sped up. Neel broke into a sprint, praying he wouldn't drop the cub. Was that their own father chasing them?

"Ay-yo!" That was Rupa!

Neel turned to see his sister down on her hands and knees. "Didi! Are you OK?"

"I tripped! It's my stupid sari! You go! I'll delay them!" Quickly she lay down face-first, her body sprawled across the path.

Neel threw his sister one last desperate look before racing toward the tamarind tree. He could hear men shouting, and then the voices stopped. They must have reached Rupa. How would she explain being out alone at night, facedown on the path, wet and dirty? Would she manage to buy the time he needed to jump into the boat? Even if he made it to the boat, how could he hold the cub *and* row to the reserve, now that he was on his own?

The cub's heart was beating fast, too. She was as scared as he was. He had to get her to safety! If she were caught now, she'd be dead before morning. He dashed along the path through the huts and rice paddies, over the small bridges, his breath coming in gasps. He raced past the tamarind tree and worksite for Gupta's house. Almost there!

"Stop!"

Neel didn't obey. It wasn't Baba's voice. He was to the dock now, almost to the place where his father's *nauka* was secured. But it was too late! Three men caught up to him, and he spun around to face them. He recognized their faces in the moonlight—Gupta's foreman, Viju's father, and one of the bricklayers who had been working on the site. And there was Viju, cowering behind his father. But where was Baba?

For a quick second Neel pictured himself breaking through the triangle of pursuers, leaping into the *nauka*, and rowing himself and the cub away from danger.

But before he could move, the foreman grabbed his shirt and lifted his stick high over Neel's head. Neel shielded the cub and braced for the blow. He wouldn't hand the cub over without a fight—he couldn't.

"It's only a boy—my carpenter's son." It was Gupta, waddling over to the dock. Viju's father, Viju, and the bricklayer backed away to make room for Gupta, but the foreman didn't budge.

Gupta shone a bright flashlight across Neel's face and arms. "He has the cub! How lovely! Well done, well done. But why are you holding the boy like that, stupid fellow?"

"He didn't stop when we told him to," the foreman growled, but he lowered his stick and let go of Neel's shirt.

Then Neel caught sight of Baba—his own father—striding to the dock. In the past that sight would have reassured Neel and made him feel safe, but now he wasn't sure, couldn't be sure, and he didn't try to stop the tears.

"That's my son!" Baba pushed his way through the men to stand beside Gupta. Neel flinched when he saw the shock on his father's face.

"Brains run in the family, I see," Gupta said, clapping Baba on the back. "You and your boy will get the whole reward, no doubt about that. Now hand the cub over, Son."

Neel clutched the cub even tighter. "She belongs on the reserve with her mother," he said. He kept his eyes on Baba. "I'm taking her to the rangers."

Viju gasped. The foreman and bricklayer grunted threats and stepped forward.

"Don't you want that reward, Son?" Gupta asked, still smiling. "It's a lot of money for a boy like you."

"Many things in life are worth more than money," Neel said.

Gupta's smile disappeared. "Take the cub," he said. "That's his father's job," the foreman grunted.

Baba came toward Neel. Would his father take the cub? Would he order Neel to hand her over? The small creature nestled closer, and Neel choked out the words: "Please, Baba, please."

For a long minute Baba looked into Neel's eyes, then down at the cub. Suddenly he whirled to face Gupta. "Neel, get into the *nauka* and wait for me." Baba's voice was steady, but he was clutching his *sundari* stick.

Neel obeyed, his heart racing. Somehow he managed to leap into the *nauka* with the cub safely in his arms. The vessel swayed with the jolt of his landing.

"What are you doing?" It was the foreman.

"We've been hunting for that cub night and day, Jai," added Viju's father. "Have you lost your senses?"

"I've come back to my senses," Baba answered.

"I'll make you give her to us!" the foreman shouted, leaping forward and swinging his pole at Baba.

Neel cried out, but Baba met the blow with his hand-carved *sundari* stick. *Thwack!* The other man's weapon shattered into pieces.

Gupta stepped forward. "No need for violence.

I'll double the reward if your son hands over the cub to us. And then we'll forget this . . . er, incident . . . ever happened."

Baba glanced over his shoulder at Neel, who was watching from the boat. "Your men would have to beat me *and* my son before you take that cub."

There was a silence. Baba didn't budge.

Finally Gupta spat in the dirt. "How dare you defy me!" he snarled. "You fool! Don't you know who I am?"

"I know exactly who you are," Baba said. He strode to the dock, leaped into the boat with Neel, untied it, and slowly, easily, began rowing across the river.

Neel held his breath. Would Gupta command his men to follow them? It sounded as if he might be trying, but none of them came to the dock. The three men stood like statues in the moonlight, watching Baba, Neel, and the cub cross the river. Behind them, Viju raised a hand and waved it quickly, and Neel waved back.

Gupta's silhouette stomped off toward his house. What would he do to Baba? Could he do anything to their family? Neel didn't know, and right now he didn't care. He was with Baba in his *nauka*—and they were rowing the cub to safety.

fourteen

"Is Didi OK?" Neel asked as soon as they were out of earshot of the shore.

"When we caught up with her, she seemed to be in a daze. She didn't say much, but muttered something about sleepwalking, which bought you a bit more time. I had to escort her home. A fine actress, that sister of yours. She should think about starring in a Bollywood film."

Neel grinned and dropped another kiss on the cub's head. She'd fallen asleep. Her tiny body rose and fell with each milky, warm breath.

Baba stopped rowing and reached over to stroke

the cub's fur with his big hand. "I wonder what the rangers call her," he said.

"I'd name her Sundari if she were mine," Neel said. "Little beauty" suited the cub perfectly.

"That's right, Son. What a way with words you have."

They traveled the rest of the way without speaking, but this time the silence between them wasn't heavy, like it had been during those troubled meals. Instead the quiet of the Sunderbans encircled them like the salty, warm night air. Baba rowed smoothly, and when they crossed the halfway point, he began singing like all the fishermen did when they neared the reserve. Rumor had it that songs kept the tigers from attacking. Neel joined in. Together, he and Baba sang their way across the moonlit waterway.

The dock that was used by the rangers was sturdy and long, reaching into the deep water. Two motor patrol boats, tied and locked securely, bobbed in the water as Baba's *nauka* bumped into the dock. At the end of the dock was a high chain-link gate and the fence that surrounded the ranger station. Nylon mesh was attached to it, stretching out on either side for miles and miles to keep the tigers inside the reserve.

As Baba moored the *nauka*, Neel climbed carefully

out, still cradling the cub. He followed Baba up the dock as fast as he could, trying not to wake her.

"Open up!" Baba called, banging the gate with his stick. They couldn't stay outside the fence for long; not with a frantic mother trying her best to escape from the reserve and find her cub. Their presence and the cub's scent might be just enough for the angry tiger to break through the fence and attack them.

Lights came on in the windows of the ranger station. "Who's there?" a voice called.

"We have the cub!" Neel called.

A door flew open; the cub started in Neel's arms. A ranger shone his flashlight on their faces and then fumbled with his keys. The gate swung open, and they were safely inside. "You're that boy we met on the path a few days ago, aren't you?" It was Kushal, the head ranger who had spoken with Headmaster.

"Yes, sir, I am. You told me to bring the cub to you, remember?"

Carefully, gently, Neel handed the now-alert cub to the ranger. His arms felt strangely empty as they dangled by his side.

"God has heard our prayers," said Kushal, stroking the cub's head as he held her. "We've been frantic with worry—the other rangers are on your island right now. We heard rumors about a bounty on her head. Is that true?"

Neel suddenly remembered Gupta's ugly threat. Would they get into even more trouble if they told the truth?

But Baba straightened his shoulders and then lifted his chin. "That new fellow on our island—Gupta—he offered a reward for the cub. I'm sure he intended to sell the creature on the black market."

Kushal shook his head. "We've been tracking that man's poaching and logging activities for some time now. The police are quite interested in him also, for other reasons. This might be the very piece of information we need to get him out of the Sunderbans once and for all. Would you be willing to testify against him?"

Baba smiled at Neel—his old, familiar smile. "Definitely," he said.

"We'll move quickly. I'll try to get the police there as soon as I can." The ranger turned to Neel. "Is the cub hurt in any way?"

"No, she was hiding inside a cave. I think she's fine. Wants her mother, though, that's for sure."

"And how her mother wants her! She almost escaped

again yesterday, but we managed to keep her inside without having to tranquilize her. She's been prowling tonight on the other side of the fence, with her other cub close by. There she is now—hear that?"

A loud growl came from the darkness behind the ranger station. The cub lifted her head, twitched her ears, and answered her mother with a soft mew.

"Can't you take her to them now?" Neel asked. "She drank a lot of goat's milk—almost a whole bucket full."

Kushal smiled. "I can see that. And smell it, too. Is that how you lured her to you?"

Neel wrinkled his nose. Rain, mud, tiger, and goat's milk—he needed a bath! "It was my sister's idea," he said.

"A smart pair, the both of you." He cocked his head. "I hear the boat; the other rangers must have given up. Come, let's show them your find, shall we?"

Two rangers, muddy and bleary-eyed after a long night of searching, crowded around the cub. They touched her gently, took photos, and thanked Neel and his father again and again.

"That's enough," Kushal said finally. "Her mother's waiting anxiously. Let me scan the cub for any wounds or bites before we release her. We need to tell head-quarters we've found her."

As Kushal checked the cub carefully from head to tail, one of the rangers radioed a message while the other sat in front of the computer. Baba sat down to wait, while Neel walked around the office. Books and newspapers were scattered across the desk, and Neel's eye was drawn to them immediately. A few expensive-looking books written in English looked untouched, their covers shiny, full of words and pictures waiting to be discovered.

"What are those about?" Baba asked him.

Neel read the few titles aloud, struggling to translate them into Bangla for his father. "*Project Tiger. Deforestation and Cyclones: A Deadly Combination. Flora and Fauna of the Mangrove Forest. Endangered Species in the Bay of Bengal. Asian Honeybees of the Sunderbans.*"

"Good to know so many fine minds are working to protect this place," Baba said. Then he glanced at Neel. "But I wonder if any of these scholars and authors grew up here, like you, Son."

It was a good question. The cover of the first book featured a photograph of a tiger peering through the mangrove trees. Could an outsider—even an Indian one—understand this place half as well as someone born and raised here? Someone who, say, had actually held a baby tiger cub in his arms? Neel was sure he'd find plenty of mistakes inside these books if he ever got the chance to read them. His fingers itched to turn the pages.

Kushal looked up from the cub. "She's fine," he said, and Neel could hear the relief in his voice.

"She certainly is," Baba said. "Does she have a name?"

"Not yet. We've been arguing about what to call her for weeks." He turned to Neel. "Maybe you have a suggestion?"

"Sundari," Neel said quickly. "She's Sundari."

The rangers laughed. "I like it," the one at the computer said.

"And you deserve to name her," added the other.

"I see you like the look of those books, Son," Kushal said, smiling. "Headmaster said you read English well. He's a good man, but strict to the core, isn't he?"

"Very strict," said Neel and his father together, and all five of them laughed.

"Why don't you take those books home with you? I've managed to get through most of them, and you deserve some kind of reward."

"Really? I can have them?" Neel had never owned a book of his own.

"They're yours. Read them, and keep studying. We need all the help we can get to keep this reserve going. A smart boy like you could do a lot of good for this place if you keep doing well in your studies."

Neel caught Baba's eye. "I'll try, sir. I'll give it a try."

"Good. Let's go reunite this baby with her mother, shall we?"

Kushal led them to the back of the station. A small gate in the high chain-link fence led out into open tiger territory. "There they are," he said. "See them?"

He was pointing into a grove about fifty meters from the fence. The moon was higher now and not as bright, but Neel squinted into the trees. Suddenly he glimpsed the tigress, pacing back and forth. She must have caught sight of them just as he saw her, because she slipped back into the darkness of the trees.

"I don't see the other baby," Neel said.

"Oh, he's there—don't worry. Hiding in the shadows, just behind his mother. I'll let the cub out now. You may wish her well, if you'd like."

The cub's eyes were open, and this time both her nose and her ears were twitching. Baba and the other two rangers each stroked Sundari's fur. Neel leaned over and dropped a last kiss on the small head. *Good-bye, little friend! You've traveled far from your home, but now you're back. Peace be with you!*

Cradling the cub, Kushal walked across the yard to the fence and unlocked and opened the gate. He set the cub down outside the fence and then quickly closed and locked the gate again.

Baba put his hand on Neel's shoulder. With a little bound and no backward look, Sundari raced toward her mother and brother. The mother tiger and the other baby must have caught the cub's scent, because suddenly they came out into the open. The three creatures became one ecstatic tangle of golden, white, and black fur, cavorting in the moonlight.

fifteen

WHEN THEIR NAUKA returned to the dock on their island, Neel was relieved to see that nobody was waiting for them. "Baba, will Gupta try to get revenge?" he asked as they walked slowly up the path toward home. They were lugging the five heavy books the ranger had given Neel, and Baba was also carrying their decoy masks and his long, sturdy stick.

"I'm sure he's angry," Baba answered. "But you heard the ranger—they've been looking for a way to get him off our island. Sounds like he can't risk breaking any more laws."

"But you've lost your carpentry job, Baba."

Baba shrugged. "We managed to make ends meet before I worked for Gupta, didn't we?"

Neel nodded. They were almost home, and he was suddenly so tired he could hardly keep his eyes open. But Rupa was waiting in the courtyard. She jumped to her feet when she spotted them. "What happened? What happened? Where's the cub?"

As she heard about the foreman's stick, Gupta's response, and the cub's joyous reunion with her mother, Rupa's eyes filled. Bending, she touched Baba's feet and then her own forehead in a *pranam*—the gesture of honor younger people gave elders on special occasions. Baba handed Neel the books he was holding and placed his hand on Rupa's head in the traditional response. "Make sure you don't 'sleepwalk' again, my daughter," he said, smiling. "I'm going inside to tell your mother the news."

Rupa threw her arms around Neel. "You did it!"

"*We* did it, you mean," Neel said. And then he yawned so widely that he almost fell over.

"Straight to the pump to wash. And then to bed. Here, give me those books. How did you get them?"

"That ranger Kushal gave them to me. They're all about the Sunderbans."

She weighed the heaviest one in her hand. "I wish I could read them, too."

Neel felt a rush of love for his sister. Rupa deserved to study and learn as much as he did. She was right, and so was the ranger—there *were* certain things that had to change in the Sunderbans. "I'll tell you what they say," he promised.

"After you win that scholarship," she said firmly. "Math certainly came in handy when you drew that map of the island, didn't it? Think you might study any harder now?"

Neel smiled, yawned again, and stumbled sleepily across the courtyard to the pump. As dirty as he was, he almost hated to scrub away the smells of musky tiger cub, souring goat's milk, thick creek mud, and salty Sunderbans water.

Morning came fast. Neel felt as though he'd barely closed his eyes before it was time for breakfast. While the family ate, Baba, Neel, and Rupa described the previous night's events to a bewildered Ma.

"Did you get any reward for turning in the cub?" she asked Neel.

"Yes, Ma, I did." Neel proudly showed her the five beautiful books the ranger had given him.

"That's my smart boy!" she exclaimed, caressing the book covers with one hand and his cheek with the other.

She turned suddenly to Baba. "But won't Gupta's men come after you?"

"Let them," Baba said, smiling at Neel. "A man's body can bear a beating, but if his soul is damaged . . ."

"That sounds well and good, Husband, but who will provide for us if something happens to you?"

A shadow crossed Baba's face. "I still have to earn money to hire that tutor," he said.

"But I'm going to study harder now, Baba!" Neel cried. "I promise!"

"He will, Baba," Rupa added. "He's starting to understand a lot of math. I've actually seen him put his skills to use."

"The tutor isn't your worry, children," Ma said. "Your father and I will discuss it. It's almost time for school, Neel. Go change or you'll be late."

Neel slowly went inside to put on his uniform. Even if he did study his hardest, would he be able to catch up on the math he needed to solve the problems on the exam? Maybe he *did* need a tutor. But how could they pay for one, especially now that Baba had no chance of earning anything from Gupta? Suddenly Neel's eye fell on the beautiful chair and desk Baba had built so carefully, and an idea leaped into his mind.

Hmm . . . , he thought, *I think I know of one carpentry job on the island. It might be worth a try.*

Baba came inside. "I'm glad you found that cub, Son," he said slowly. "I can't tell you how glad. And I do believe you'll try your best to study in the time you have left. But there isn't much, and we still need to hire a tutor. I'll head to Kolkata this afternoon to find carpentry work."

"Maybe I do need a tutor, Baba," Neel said, "but I have another plan—let me give it a try before you leave the island."

Baba listened as Neel explained, and then he laughed out loud. "He can only say no. I suppose I can wait until you find out."

Neel tucked the map into his pocket and swung his satchel over his shoulder. Baba handed him the small chair he had so lovingly built and carved.

"Don't say anything to Ma or Didi," Neel said. "I want to bring home the good news—if there is any." Slipping out of the courtyard so his mother and Rupa wouldn't spot him, he hurried to school.

sixteen

AJAY WAS WAITING impatiently by the well. "Viju told me about your adventures last night! And how you and your *baba* stood up to Gupta! I wish I could have been there!"

"The foreman's pole shattered right when it smashed into Baba's strong stick! You should have seen it!"

"Tell me everything—from start to finish!"

Neel recounted the whole story as they walked to school, prompted by eager questions from his friend.

"I hope the police arrest Gupta soon," Ajay said. "He's going to come after your *baba* and get his revenge."

"Baba's not worried," Neel answered. "And the ranger said they'd move quickly."

"Why in the world are you bringing that chair to school?" Ajay asked.

"I'm going to show it to Headmaster," Neel said.

"What? Why? You're going to barge into his office to show him a *chair*? Are you crazy?"

Again, Neel explained his idea.

Ajay's smile faded. "So now you actually *want* to win that scholarship?"

"I do. I've got to give it a try, Ajay."

"Oh, well. You still might not win. That's what I'm hoping for, anyway."

His friend was right: Neel might place second, or third, or last. But everything had changed because of the cub's rescue. He wanted to take good care of her, of his island, and even the rest of the Sunderbans. For the first time since Headmaster had sent that letter, he was going to do his best to win.

Neel went straight to Headmaster's office as soon as they arrived. "Hope you come out alive," Ajay called as he headed for the classroom.

I hope so, too. Neel gathered his courage. He was a tiger hunter, after all, wasn't he? He took a deep breath and knocked at the door.

"Come in," the familiar voice barked from inside.

Neel opened the door. "Good morning, sir," he said, walking up to the desk.

Headmaster ignored him. He was concentrating on a letter that he'd apparently opened hastily, judging by the ripped envelope. Headmaster read to the end and then read it all the way through again before looking up. Then, to Neel's amazement, he smiled, stood up, and came around his desk. "You saved that cub, boy?"

Neel put down the chair with a thud. "I did, sir."

"Kushal had the news hand-delivered to me this morning by *nauka*. Apparently that Gupta man is gone. Vanished in the night."

"So quickly? The rangers and police can't catch him?"

Headmaster shook his head. "He fled in the night. Must have guessed that your father would testify about his poaching attempt."

"He knows everyone trusts Baba's word," Neel said.

"That is true, Neel. Even as a student, your *baba* never lied to anybody, and an honest witness often brings more shady activities into the light. Gupta may find a way to make trouble somewhere else, but he won't come back to the Sunderbans. But back to you and the cub—how in the world did you guess where she was hiding?"

"I've played hide-and-seek around here for years,

sir." Neel dug into his pocket and pulled out the map. "So while I was drawing this, I remembered a few places that I thought nobody else knew about."

Headmaster unfolded the graph paper. He studied Neel's map for what seemed like a long time. "Astoundingly accurate," he murmured, turning the paper upside down and studying it some more. "Not bad, not bad at all. And why are you bringing me a chair?"

Neel rested his hand on the smooth wood of the chair's back. "I'm not bringing it to you, sir. I'm only displaying it. My *baba* made it for me, and I can sit easily for hours on it to study. Have a look."

"Your father made that?" Headmaster fingered the intricate carving around the chair's back, the shining *sundari* wood, the careful joints and brackets that held the sturdy legs in place. Then he glanced back at his own small, rickety desk and stiff, uncomfortable chair. "It *is* nicely crafted. Perhaps there is more to Jai than I realized. But why should this matter to me now?"

"Baba has agreed to build you a beautiful, comfortable new desk and chair, sir. He will measure you from head to toe. Then he will use *sundari* wood from our trees to build your new furniture to fit you perfectly. It will be strong and will last for a long time."

"And why would your *baba* do this for me?"

Neel took a deep breath. It was time to unveil his entire idea. "He will build you this desk and chair in exchange for your help, sir. He humbly requests that you take on the job of tutoring me in math."

"Me? Ha! You must be thinking of that fellow in Kolkata—the miracle worker. You are growling up the wrong bush, my boy, as the English like to say."

For the first time, Neel didn't hold back his correction. "I think you mean 'barking up the wrong tree,' sir," he said.

"Yes, yes, that's what I meant. How dare you correct me, boy? Aren't you asking for my help?"

"Pardon me, Headmaster. But our family can't afford that tutor from Kolkata, sir, and I've heard you say that math was your best subject. I think I could learn it now—with your help."

Headmaster gave Neel a searching look. "Well, if I did take on a student—which I haven't done in years, mind you—I certainly wouldn't waste my time teaching someone who doesn't want that scholarship . . . or have you changed your mind?"

"Yes, sir, I have. I would like very much to win that scholarship now."

"Why?"

How could he explain his change of heart? Images flew through his mind—his sister sweeping the floor, glancing every now and then at his books and papers; Baba's strong hand resting on his head; Sundari racing across the reserve to her mother in the shelter of the trees that shared her name; the ranger's reward of five books waiting to be read, maybe even corrected and improved.

"I didn't want to leave the Sunderbans, sir," he said slowly. "But I see now that I might have to, to learn how to keep the good things here good—for us, and for the trees, and the animals—and maybe even make some things better."

"True. Very true." Headmaster turned to gaze at the schoolyard, where Class Two students were standing in rows and reciting their spelling lessons.

"I'll come back, though, sir." Neel had to say it. "I won't be like the others who go to study at that school and never come home."

"Not all of the scholarship winners leave for good," Headmaster said, still looking out the window. "One did come back. The last boy from our island who won, in fact."

"Really, sir? Who was that?"

Headmaster turned around. He was smiling. "Me."

Neel tried not to show his surprise. "You, sir?"

Headmaster smiled again. "I've been hoping for another winner from our school for years. I thought you might be a possibility from the moment you enrolled. I left my books and magazines in the library so you could keep reading. Your scores in reading and writing were superb, and I almost danced with joy. But you were always weaker in math, and when you stopped trying altogether, I didn't know what to do."

Neel remembered the reading material that used to appear in the library. *Headmaster* was the magician? It was hard to believe, but somehow now it made sense. "My lack of effort is over now, sir. I promise to try my hardest. We still have some time, sir. Will you teach me?" Neel risked a smile. "Besides, the headmaster of our school needs a fine new chair and desk, doesn't he?"

"Perhaps he does, perhaps he does. But it would be a much bigger 'bird's wing on my hat' if you won that scholarship. All right, Neel, we have a deal."

Feather in your cap. He didn't say it aloud this time;

there was a right moment for corrections, and this wasn't it. "You won't regret it, sir—I promise."

"Get ready for a course of intensive mathematics. Every day after school. You are going to master geometry and algebra if it is the last thing I do."

seventeen

THE GOOD NEWS was that Gupta had disappeared. Nobody knew where he'd gone. His half-finished house stood by the tamarind tree, the only trace left of the big man from the city who had tried to take over their island.

Viju's father went back to fishing and would hunt honey when it came in season, and Viju came back sheepishly for the last few weeks of school. "I might as well graduate from Class Five with you two dummies," he told his friends.

Ajay and Neel welcomed him back, and so did Headmaster. "You have only two more months left of instruction in this school," he told all the Class Five students. "Make the best of them."

Neel would never forget those long days of studying, spending hours first in the classroom, then in Headmaster's office, and finally at his desk at home. Math, math, and more math. Sometimes Headmaster got frustrated and crumpled up Neel's papers, and his red pen flew like a carving knife as he made endless corrections. Other times he made Neel solve the same problem ten times until he was sure Neel understood it. A few times he lost his temper, shouted, and stamped out of the room in disgust. But he always came back.

Meanwhile Neel sweated, groaned, and came close to tears a number of times. This was the hardest thing he'd done in his life, he decided—much harder than fleeing from a would-be poacher in the middle of the night. The steady, persistent mastery of math required more courage and endurance than that one night had demanded—more than he could muster on his own. But as Neel had anticipated, Headmaster turned out to be a top-notch math teacher despite his impatience. He pulled, pushed, and prodded, and Neel struggled and practiced and memorized, until slowly the mysteries of algebra and geometry managed to untangle in his brain.

Baba delivered a tailor-made *sundari* desk and chair to the school the day before the exam. "This is excellent craftsmanship, Jai," Headmaster said, sitting comfortably in his new chair. "If I can raise enough funds, I might hire you to build new desks for the whole school."

"I'd do it, sir," Baba said. "But you'll have to provide the wood from outside. My trees need some time to grow back their branches. And I won't cut down any *sundari* trees in the reserve."

"Nor should you. We'll find you some good wood elsewhere. I'm getting close to convincing a few key people to invest in our school. Now, Neel, how are you feeling about tomorrow?"

"Can't wait until the exam is over, sir."

"Just as I felt when I took it," Headmaster said. "They'll send me the results here in due time, and I'll come to your house with the news, good or bad. Get a good night's sleep tonight."

For once, words weren't enough. Bowing, Neel touched Headmaster's feet and then his own forehead in a *pranam* of respect. In return, Headmaster placed his hand on Neel's head in a gesture of blessing.

The following morning Neel and Baba said good-bye to Ma and Rupa and then boarded the ferry to the regional scholarship examination center. Students streamed in from villages all across the Sunderbans and took their seats in straight rows. Proctors strode up and down the aisles as they administered the exam.

Baba sipped cups of tea and chatted with the other parents while Neel took the four-hour test. "How was it?" Baba asked when Neel emerged. "English and Bangla were easy, I know, but how was the math?"

"I finished all the problems, at least," Neel said.

"Well, it's done, anyway. Now it's time for a rest, Son. You've worked hard."

Neel, Ajay, and Viju thoroughly enjoyed that holiday. They played cricket, swam in the pond, and even organized a few games of hide-and-seek for the smaller children in the village. At the end of the hot season, Viju would join his father full-time on his fishing boat or leave with him for Chennai. No more school for him—he was done for good. Ajay would head to the secondary school on a nearby island and keep muddling along for a few more years of schooling. "Until my *baba* finally gives up on me," he said ruefully. Neel would either join Ajay or travel all the way to Kolkata to enroll in St. James Secondary

Boarding School—if he won the scholarship, that is. He tried not to think about it, and they didn't talk much about it at home, but he knew the whole family was waiting for Headmaster's visit.

One hot April afternoon, while Neel's family was resting outside in the shade, Gupta's ex-foreman appeared in the courtyard. He stood gazing up at the *sundari* trees, and Baba rose to greet him, with Neel following close behind.

"May we help you?" Baba asked.

"I came to ask for exactly that," the man said. "I'm planting some *sundari* trees on my property, and I want to know where to place them to protect my paddies and pepper field. I live on the next island, and the cyclone hit there almost as hard as it did here. Could you advise me?"

"Gladly," Baba said. "I'll bring my *nauka* to your place tomorrow. But please wait here for one moment." He disappeared inside and came out carrying his finest *sundari* pole. "Here, take this. I'm sorry I broke your pole that night."

The man smiled sheepishly as he took Baba's gift. "This one is much stronger than the one I had. I'll see you tomorrow."

The next afternoon, while Baba was out fulfilling his promise, the family had another visitor. It was Headmaster, out of breath and drenched in sweat. Neel, Ma, and Rupa were in the courtyard, and they all leaped to their feet at the sight of him.

Neel's heart skipped a beat. Headmaster had said he'd come with good news—or bad.

"Get me some water, will you, Rupa?" Headmaster asked. "Hotter than ever on this cursed island, isn't it?"

Rupa brought the water while Neel tugged a chair into the shade. Ma brought out a big banana leaf and began fanning Headmaster.

"Where is your father, Neel?" Headmaster asked after chugging the water in one gulp.

"He'll be home shortly, sir," Neel said. And then he risked it: "Do you have news about the exam, sir?"

Headmaster smiled. "I do," he said. He stood up and faced Neel. "I wanted to tell your father, but maybe you deserve to hear it first. You scored higher than any boy from the Sunderbans in English and Bangla."

"Ay-yo!" Ma said, and then clapped her hand over her mouth. Neel could tell that Rupa was still holding her breath.

"What about math, sir?" he asked.

"Well, you didn't do that badly in math either," Headmaster said, clapping Neel on the shoulders with both hands. "Not the highest score in the region, by any means, but just high enough."

"High enough?" Neel asked. "High enough for what, sir?"

"To win that scholarship, Neel!"

"*Dhanyabad, Bhogoban!*" Ma shouted, throwing her arms in the air to thank God. "*Dhanyabad!*"

With a thud Neel plunked down on the chair Headmaster had vacated, the chair crafted so lovingly by Baba, the chair that had carried him through those long, long hours of studying.

"I knew you would win, Neel!" Rupa crowed, joy spreading like honey across her face.

Ma was wiping her tears away with the end of her sari. "Neel, hurry! Go meet your *baba*—he should be returning by now. And bring sweets, too. Rupa, bring Headmaster some tea. And then go tell the neighbors our good news!"

Neel sprinted as fast as he could along the path. He was almost out of breath when he reached the dock, but there was Baba, mooring his *nauka*. "Baba, I won! I won the scholarship!"

Baba dropped the rope and lifted both hands high. "I knew it! That's my boy!"

Neel grabbed the rope before the *nauka* could drift away and secured it to the dock. On the way home, Baba called the news to everybody they passed. He stopped at the shack to buy a big clay bowl of sweets. When they got home, Headmaster was still sitting in the shade, mopping his forehead and sipping a cup of tea.

"This is all your doing, sir." Baba bent to give Headmaster a *pranam* of respect, but Headmaster stopped him.

"Stand up, stand up, Jai. You raised this fine boy; all the credit goes to you."

Ma was still crying with happiness, the goats bleated, chickens crowed and clucked, and neighbors began gathering to share the joy. Baba, beaming with pride, handed out the *rôshogolla* treats to their visitors.

Rupa was out in the garden gathering marigolds, the flowers of victory, to make Neel a garland. When it was done, she flung it over his head.

"I'll come home, Didi," he told her in a low voice. "I'll make sure you get to study, too."

"I know you will," she said. "And then I'll catch up to you before you know it."

"Maybe you'll pass me," he said, and she smiled.

She placed a big basket of extra blooms nearby, so that others could use them to make garlands. As neighbors and family members clapped him on the back or tossed strings of flowers around his neck, Neel glanced at the *sundari* trees. They were standing still and silent in the heat, shading the crowd of happy people from the blaze of sunshine.

He thought of the tiger cub growing stronger in her reserve, safe for now from poachers, playing with her brother and learning to hunt. Like his sister, like the trees, like all of the Sunderbans, she would wait for his return.

I won't let you down, Neel promised them all silently, and then ducked. Ajay and Viju had appeared out of nowhere, hooting, shouting, and pelting him with marigolds.

Author's Note

Take a three-hour drive from the bustling Indian city of Kolkata—my birthplace—and you'll arrive at an archipelago of islands called the Sunderbans (also spelled "Sundarbans"). It's a mysterious, one-of-a-kind mangrove forest, home to trees that send roots up instead of down for oxygen, animals and plants that can survive on salty water, and the only wild tigers on the planet that eat people.

This delta area of tidal rivers, mudflats, creeks, and islands spans two countries—India and Bangladesh. The Indian side in the state of West Bengal is made up of 102 islands, with people living on 54 of them. The rest of the islands are set apart as a mangrove forest preserve and are home to the last remaining wild Bengal tigers in the world.

Everything in the Sunderbans is trying hard to survive—tigers, trees, people, and even the soil itself. The islands are shrinking thanks to deforestation, cyclones, and erosion. This causes suffering for both tigers and human beings, and sometimes results in conflict between them.

One problem is people attacking tigers. The Indian government has cracked down on poaching, but tiger body parts are still wanted on the black market to make medicine. In addition, people around the world desire tiger pelts for decoration. The demand for dead tigers creates a temptation to supply them.

Another problem is tigers attacking people. One tiger needs about twenty-five thousand acres of habitat to survive. If animal prey isn't available, human beings become a possible source of food. Some estimate that about fifty to sixty villagers are killed each year by tigers. Meanwhile, people living in the Sunderbans are hungry, too. Erosion means they don't have as much land to farm. To make things worse, every year or two, cyclones rage up from the Bay of Bengal and devastate homes and crops. Men and women venture into the Sunderbans preserve to fish, catch crabs, and gather honey for their families, leaving them open to attacks by tigers.

People. Animals. Land. Trees. Climate. Greed. Hunger. Need. All these elements converge to create a cyclone of struggle in the Sunderbans. The survival of the village communities, the majestic Bengal tiger, and other endangered species depend on a concerted global effort. This book is my way of inviting us to become part of a solution.

Acknowledgments

I'd like to thank the staff of the US Consulate in Kolkata and our friends Dean and Jane Thompson. Dean was serving as the US Consul General during the research phase of this book, and his staff organized a trip to the Sunderbans. Thanks to them I was able to interview experts such as Biswajit Roy Chowdhury and Ajanta Dey of Nature Environment and Wildlife Society, Sunderbans Tiger Reserve Field Director Soumitra Dasgupta, and rangers at the Sajnekhali watchtower in the Sunderbans Tiger Reserve. We also enjoyed the hospitality of community members participating in a mangrove plantation project on Amtoli Island.

This story would not be here if it hadn't been for Yolanda Scott, who steered and nurtured the process (and me) via lunches, coffees, and gentle emails. *Tiger Boy* was conceived as a small idea and became a book only because of the expert midwifery of this brilliant, caring editor. Thanks also go to the whole Charlesbridge team, a dedicated group of literary cheerleaders.

My husband, Rob, continues to be the patron of my art. He provides shelter and sustenance, encouragement when I get stuck, and steadfast faith in my vocation. He accompanied me to Bengal during my research because he loves my *desh* (home country) as much as I do. Thanks to him, we recently moved back to California so that I could continue to write while spending more time with my beloved parents, sisters, and sons, James and Timothy.

My parents, Sailendra Nath and Madhusree Bose, told me

stories about growing up in the villages of Bengal, and Dad, in particular, shared memories of tides, boats, and fishing. Last but certainly not least, many of my writing themes emerge from reflection on the parables of Jesus. This book is based on the story about the talents given to three stewards (Matthew 25:14–30).

Organizations Working with Bengal Tigers

Project Tiger is the branch of the Indian government responsible for safe-guarding the tiger population.
http://projecttiger.nic.in/

Panthera is "devoted exclusively to the conservation of the world's 37 species of wild cats and their ecosystems."
http://www.panthera.org/species/tiger

Panthera and Save the Tiger Fund joined forces in 2011 to address the many challenges facing wild tigers.
http://www.panthera.org/programs/tiger/save-tiger-fund

World Wildlife Fund, an independent conservation organization, works in more than one hundred countries to "stop the degradation of the planet's natural environment and to build a future in which humans live in harmony with nature."
https://worldwildlife.org/species/bengal-tiger

Organizations Working to Improve Life in the Sunderbans

Nature Environment and Wildlife Society (NEWS) protects and conserves wildlife, ecology, and the environment. NEWS engages people dependent on threatened ecosystems to enhance the conservation process.
http://www.naturewildlife.org

World Vision Asia's "Our Forest, Our Life: A Community-based Action Towards the Sustainability of the Sundarbans Reserve Forest (CBAS-SRF)" improves the biodiversity of the forest and reduces the risk of disaster. http://www.wvi.org/bangladesh/cbas-project

Save the Children builds the preparedness, response capacity, and resilience of children, communities, and local governance in the Sundarbans.
https://bangladesh.savethechildren.net

Partners International Canada is a Christian nonprofit specializing in holistic transformation and long-term sustainable international development.
http://partnersinternational.ca/sponsor/adopt-an-island/

Glossary

Auntie: A term of respect used in India and Bangladesh to refer to or address any older woman.

Baba: A name that children call their father in many languages, including Bengali, Arabic, Chinese, and Greek.

ban: The Bangla word for "tidal bore."

Bangla/Bengali: The language of Bengal, which includes Bangladesh and the Indian states of West Bengal, Tripura, and southern Assam. About 250 million people speak Bangla, making it the seventh most spoken language in the world.

bangle: A traditional bracelet worn by women in India, Pakistan, and Bangladesh. Girls begin wearing bangles when they are toddlers.

Bollywood: The Hindi-language film industry based in Mumbai, India. This term is often used to refer to the whole of India's film industry.

Bon Bibi: The Hindu and Muslim guardian spirit of the residents of the Sunderbans. She is often called upon to protect against attacks from tigers.

Chennai: The capital city of Tamil Nadu, a state in the southern part of India. It is located off the Bay of Bengal, about 1500 kilometers (900 miles) from the Sunderbans.

chup: A sound used by an elder to warn a child that they should be quiet or watch what they say.

cricket field: The field on which the popular game of cricket is played. The game was created in the United Kingdom, is enjoyed widely throughout South Asia, and involves a wide bat-like paddle, a ball, and two teams.

"Dhanyabad, Bhogoban": "Thank you, God" in Bangla.

didi: "Older sister" in Bangla and Hindi.

dowry: A payment of money or gifts from a bride's family to a groom's family. It may include cash, jewelry, appliances, furniture, bedding, dishes, or other household items to help the couple set up a home.

dysentery: A treatable sickness that can involve diarrhea, fever, and stomach pains, often caused by a virus, bacteria, or parasite in water or food. In extreme cases people suffer nausea, vomiting, rapid weight loss, and muscle aches. Left untreated, the sickness can also cause problems with the lungs, liver, or brain.

estuary shore: The shoreline of an estuary—a coastal water connected to the open ocean with one or more rivers or streams flowing into it. Estuaries are zones between river and ocean environments and have tides, waves, and salt water as well as fresh water and sediment.

fiddler crab: One of many species that make up the genus *Uca*. They are best known for their claws, because male fiddler crabs have one very large claw and one smaller one. (Female fiddler crabs' claws are the same size.) They mostly live along mudflats, lagoons, and swamps—areas like the Sunderbans.

frond: A large divided leaf, such as on a palm tree.

golpata: A type of palm tree native to the coastlines of the Indian and Pacific Oceans with a short trunk that grows underground and leaves and stalks that grow above ground. Commonly called a "nipa palm" (scientific name: *Nypa fruticans*), the tree is known by various regional names. "Golpata" is used in Bangladesh and West Bengal, India.

guava: A type of plant cultivated in many areas of the world that bears a fruit suitable for eating.

ilish: The national fish of Bangladesh, popular for eating throughout South Asia.

Kolkata: Also called Calcutta, the city is the capital of the state of West Bengal. It is the commercial, cultural, and educational center of eastern India and is India's oldest port city. About 4.5 million people live in the city. Kolkata is only 130 kilometers (80 miles) from the Sunderbans.

Ma: A name that children call their mother in many languages.

mangrove: A general term for a type of tree and shrub that grows on ocean coasts in the tropics and subtropics. The word can be traced back to Spanish.

marigold garland: A string of bright orange-yellow marigold flowers worn around the neck during celebrations.

nauka: The Bangla word for "boat."

neel or *nila*: The Bangla word for "blue."

pranam: Also called *pranāma* or *charana-sparśa*, this show of respect in Indian culture involves one person touching the feet of another. Children touch the feet of their elders in greeting, and people of all ages touch the feet of statues of gods.

proverb: A simple and well-known saying that expresses a commonsense or practical experience, often using a metaphor. Proverbs are borrowed across languages and cultures.

pugmark: The footprint of an animal used for identification purposes. Pugmarks are also used to track rogue animals, like the cub in the story. "Pug" means "foot" in Hindi.

reserve: A section of land set aside as a safe place for plants and animals to remain undisturbed by humans.

rhesus monkey: Also known as rhesus macaque or Nazuri monkey (scientific name: *Macaca mulatta*), it lives in a broad range of habitats and is native to most of Asia. Rhesus monkeys often live near humans.

rickshaw: Also spelled "ricksha," this is a two- or three-wheeled passenger cart generally pulled by one man with one passenger. Cycle rickshaws are pedaled and can often carry two or even three passengers. The word comes from the Japanese word for "human-powered vehicle."

rôshogolla: A cheese-based syrupy dessert of round, white, spongy sweets popular in West Bengal and Bangladesh.

rui: Also called *rohu* (scientific name: *Labeo rohita*), this carp fish is found in rivers and considered a delicacy in Bangladesh.

rupee: The name of the money used in India, Pakistan, Sri Lanka, Nepal, Mauritius, Seychelles, Maldives, and Indonesia.

sacked: A word that means being fired from a job. The term is British and is still used in countries formerly colonized by England, such as India.

sari: Also spelled "saree," this is a garment worn by girls and women in India and Bangladesh that consists of a long piece of fabric wrapped around the body with one end draped over one shoulder. A sari is usually worn over a fabric skirt and a fitted short-sleeve shirt. Saris are a symbol of Indian and Bangladeshi culture. In the story the long part of the sari is used to separate sections of the house.

sundari **stick:** A stick carved from the wood of a *sundari* tree.

sundari **tree:** The mangrove species (scientific name: *Heritiera fomes*) found in large numbers in the Sunderbans.

Sunderbans (sometimes spelled Sundarbans): A geographical area in the delta of the Bay of Bengal on the border of Bangladesh and India. The area is a UNESCO World Heritage Site and home to approximately four million people. Most of the land is for conservation, reserved to protect plants such as the mangrove and animals such as the Bengal tiger. "Sunderban" means "beautiful forest" in Bangla.

tamarind: A type of tree (scientific name: *Tamarindus indica*) with a pod-like fruit that is used around the world in cooking, as medicine, and as a metal polish. The wood of the tree can be used in carpentry. South Asia and Mexico are the largest producers and consumers of tamarind.

thali: A plastic or metal plate with sections or compartments to keep food separate.

tidal bore: A phenomenon in which an incoming tide forms a wave that travels up a river against its current.

turmeric: A plant in the ginger family. Most often the roots are boiled and dried before being ground into a deep orange-yellow powder used as a spice, for dyeing clothes, and as coloring in mustard.

133